spinning yarns

Author, poet and translator, **Deepa Agarwal** writes for both children and adults and has about fifty published books to her credit. She has received several awards for her work. The picture book, *Ashok's New Friends*, was awarded the National Award for Children's Literature by the National Council of Educational Research and Training while her historical fiction, *Caravan to Tibet*, featured in the International Board on Books for Young People Honor List of 2008. Five of her titles have also been listed in the White Raven Catalogue of the International Youth Library, Munich.

D1176737

Vaishnavi. V

48

spinning yarns

the best children's stories from india

Edited by Deepa Agarwal

RED TURTLE

RUPA

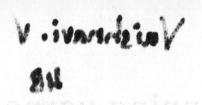

Published in Red Turtle by
Rupa Publications India Pvt. Ltd 2013
7/16, Ansari Road, Daryaganj
New Delhi 110002

Sales Centres:
Allahabad Bengaluru Chennai
Hyderabad Jaipur Kathmandu
Kolkata Mumbai

ISBN: 978-81-291-2120-2

Thirteenth impression 2022

15 14 13

Typeset in Minion Pro 12/19.2

Printed at Repro India Limited, India

contents

introduction

Go on! Dive headlong into a collection of some of the most memorable stories for children gathered together in a single book. There's something here for everyone—a gripping vampire story, thrilling adventure tales, nonsense rhymes that will tickle you silly, not to mention thought-provoking fables and fascinating fairy tales. Some stories could have been taken from your own life—stories of school and home, of celebrations and hard times, of light-hearted fun as well as heartbreak. There is a vast variety of fascinating, unforgettable characters to keep you enthralled too—clever girls, daring boys, understanding teachers and dogged shikaris.

I must confess it was not an easy task to collect these amazing stories. Indeed, when I began to think about what should be included, I realized what a daunting task

I had set myself. There was so much to choose from! It was heartwrenching to leave out some truly wonderful works because there wasn't enough space.

There are so many more memorable works, and so many writers who have created enduring classics. Tagore, Premchand, Sukumar Ray, Satyajit Ray, R.K. Narayan, have all created some unforgettable characters in Indian fiction. Pioneering writer Sukumar Ray composed some of the most hilarious nonsense rhymes ever written. I could not resist including two pieces of non-fiction—a stirring real-life adventure tale by Jim Corbett about his encounter with a dreaded man-eater, and the story of how a young girl taught her grandmother to read, by Sudha Murty.

There are many brilliant writers weaving tales for children today, writing about the problems, dreams and aspirations of today's children or carrying the reader off to mind-boggling realms of fantasy. So stories and poems by modern masters like Vikram Seth, Paul Zacharia, Sundara Ramaswamy were added to the list along with those by well-loved children's writers like Shankar, Ruskin Bond, Paro Anand and Ranjit Lal. And since ours is a large country with many languages, I collected the best from different Indian languages in translation as well—stories both old and new that have delighted and touched children who have read them in Hindi, Bengali, Malayalam and Tamil.

But why did I find these stories so special, so memorable? I felt they contained universal truths—an essential element of great writing. There are many 'A-ha!' moments in these stories. For example, Big Brother, in Premchand's story with the same name, keeps falling behind his younger brother in school, despite all his hard work. However, when he says with simple dignity, 'You are flying high today because you have stood first in your class. But you must listen to me. I may have failed but I am older than you. I have more experience of the world than you have...' Your respect for him goes up several notches—even failure has not shaken the roots of his self-belief.

The warmth of understanding floods through us when Jim Corbett states at the end of his account of a long, gruelling hunt of the man-eating tigress: 'There have been occasions when life has hung by a thread and others when a light purse and disease resulting from exposure has made the going difficult, but for all these occasions I feel amply rewarded if my hunting has resulted in saving one human life.'

These stories are rooted in our culture and history as well. We are reminded about the importance of the guru-shishya tradition in Sudha Murty's heart-warming story 'How I Taught My Grandmother to Read'. In fact, two other tales dwell on the very special relationship of grandparent and child—Shankar's fun-filled 'Rain-making' and Khushwant Singh's nostalgic 'Portrait of a Lady'.

There are many other thought-provoking themes. The power of the imagination is celebrated in Paul Zacharia's 'The Library'; and the peril of excessive attachment to worldly goods is playfully highlighted in 'Pinty's Soap'. Then there are those moments of realization, of understanding that we are all special in different ways as in 'Eid'.

There are also very real boys like Swaminathan to sympathise with when they keep getting into trouble. There are also inspirational characters like Rajappa in Sundara Ramaswamy's powerful story 'The Stamp Album', who decides to do the right thing, after doing a very wrong thing, even though it requires an enormous sacrifice.

If you adore chills, there are two goosebump-inducing stories—Satyajit Ray's scary 'The Vicious Vampire' and 'The School', Ranjit Lal's compelling tale of a very unusual school.

I felt children's writing in India should include some of the best examples of poetry for children, too. Thus the hilarious 'Mister Owl and Missus' and 'Pumpkin-Grumpkin' by Sukumar Ray. And Vikram Seth's highly entertaining 'The Goat and the Ram'.

What else can I say? That there are stories here of village life and city life, from the past and the present, set in real worlds and imaginary worlds; that this is one book you can read in one sitting or you can dip into it again and again.

So go ahead, enjoy—the road to wonderland starts right here!

Deepa Agarwal

the vicious vampire

Satyajit Ray

I have always harboured an intense dislike for bats. Whenever a flittermouse flits into my room in the house in Calcutta, I feel obliged to drop everything and rush out of the room. Particularly during the summer, I am distinctly uneasy at the thought of one of those creatures knocking against the fan spinning at full speed and dropping to the ground, hurt and injured. So I run out of my room and yell at the cook Vinod, to come and rescue me. Once, Vinod managed to kill a flittermouse with my badminton racquet. To be very honest, my dislike is often mixed with fear. The very sight of a bat puts me off. What peculiar creatures they are—neither birds nor animals, with their queer habit of hanging upside down from trees. I think that the world would have been a far

1

better place to live in if bats did not exist.

My room in Calcutta had been invaded by flittermice so many times that I had begun to think they had a strange fondness for me. But I never thought I would find a bat hanging from the ceiling in my room in this house in Shiuri. This really was too much. I could not stay in the room unless it was removed.

My father's friend, Tinkori Kaka, had told me about this house. He was a doctor and had once practised in Shiuri. After retirement, he had moved to Calcutta, but, needless to say, he still knew a lot of people in Shiuri. So I went straight to him for advice when I discovered that I would have to spend about a week there.

'Shiuri? Why Shiuri? What do you want to do there?' he asked. I told him I was working on a research project on old terracotta temples of Bengal. It was my ultimate aim to write a book on this subject. There were so many beautiful temples strewn about the country but no one had ever written a really good book on them.

'Oh, of course! You're an artist, aren't you? So your interest lies in temples, does it? But why do you want to limit yourself just to Shiuri? There are temples everywhere—Shurul, Hetampur, Dubrajpur, Phoolbera, Beersinghpur. But perhaps, those aren't good enough to be written about?'

Anyway, Tinkori Kaka told me about this house.

'You wouldn't mind staying in an old house, would you? A patient of mine used to live there. He's now shifted to Calcutta. But I believe there is a caretaker in Shiuri to look after the house. It's a fairly large place. I don't think you'll have any problem. And you wouldn't have to pay anything, either. I snatched this man back, so to speak, from the jaws of death as many as three times. He'd be only too pleased to have a guest of mine stay in his house for a week.'

Tinkori Kaka was right. There was no problem in getting to the house. But the minute I got off the cycle rickshaw that brought me from the station and entered my room, I saw the bat.

I called the old caretaker.

'What's your name?'

'Madhusudan.'

'I see. Well, then, Madhusudan—is Mr Bat a permanent resident of this room or has he come here today to give me a special welcome?'

Madhusudan looked at the ceiling, scratched his head and said, 'I hadn't noticed it, sir. This room usually stays locked. It was only opened today because you were coming.'

'But I cannot share a room with a bat.'

'Don't worry about it, sir. It will leave as soon as the sun goes down.'

'All right. But can't anything be done to make sure it doesn't return?'

'No sir. It won't come back. Why should it? After all, it's not as though it's built a nest here. It must have slipped in last night somehow and couldn't get out for it can't see during the day.'

After a cup of tea, I went and occupied an old cane chair on the veranda. The house was at one end of the town. On the northern side was a large mango grove. Through the trees it was possible to catch glimpses of rice fields that stretched right up to the horizon. On the western side was a bamboo grove and, beyond it, the spire of a church stood tall. This must be the famous ancient church of Shiuri.

I decided to walk round to the church in the evening. I should start working from tomorrow. In and around twenty-five miles of Shiuri at least thirty terracotta temples could be found. I had a camera with me and a large stock of film. Each carving on the walls of these temples should be photographed. The temples might not last very much longer and once these were destroyed, Bengal would lose an important part of its heritage.

It was now 5.30 p.m. The sun disappeared behind the church. I got up, stretched and had just taken a step toward the stairs when something flew past my left ear making swishing noise, and vanished into the mango grove.

I went into the bedroom and looked at the ceiling. The bat had gone. Thank goodness for that. At least I could work peacefully in the evening. Perhaps I should start writing about the temples I had already seen elsewhere in Burdwan, Bankura and the 24 Parganas.

As soon as darkness fell, I took out my torch and began walking towards the church. The red earth of Birbhum, the uneven terrain, the rows of palms—I loved them all. This was my first visit to Shiuri—I was not really here to look at nature and its beauty, yet the church and its surrounding struck me as beautiful. I passed the church and began walking further west. Then I saw what looked like a park. There was an open space surrounded by a railing. It had an iron gate.

As I came closer, I realized it was not a park but a graveyard. There were about thirty graves in it. A few had carved marble pillars. Others had marble slabs. All were undoubtedly quite ancient. The pillars were cracked. Little plants peeped out of some of these cracks.

The gate was open. I went in and began trying to read some of the hazy, indistinct epitaphs. All were graves of Britons, possibly those who had died in the very early stages of the Raj, as a result of some epidemic or the other.

One particular marble slab seemed to have a slightly more legible inscription. I was about to switch the torch on to read it, when I heard footsteps behind me. I turned around quickly. A short, middle-aged man was standing about ten feet away, smiling at me. He was wearing a black jacket and grey trousers. There was an old, patched up umbrella in his hand.

'You don't like bats, do you?'

I started. How did this stranger know that? The man laughed. 'You must be wondering how I found out. Very easy. When you were telling that caretaker to drive the bat away this morning, I happened to be in the vicinity.'

'Oh, I see.'

Now the man raised his hands in a namaskar.

'I am Jagdish Percival Mukherjee. My family has lived in Shiuri for a long time. Four generations, you know. I like visiting the church and this graveyard in the evening. I am a Christian, you see.'

It was getting darker. I headed back to the house. The man began walking with me. He seemed a bit strange, although he appeared to be harmless enough. But his voice was funny—thin and, at the same time, harsh. In any case, I could never be comfortable with people who made such an obvious attempt to get friendly.

I tried to switch on the torch, but it did not work. Then I remembered I had meant to buy a couple of batteries at the station, and had quite forgotten to do so. How annoying! I could not see a thing. What if there were snakes?

The man said, 'Don't worry about your torch. I am used to moving in the dark. I can see quite well. Careful— there's a pothole here!' He pulled me to one side. Then he said, 'Do you know what a vampire is?'

'Yes,' I said briefly.

Who did not know about vampires? Blood-sucking bats were called vampires. They sucked the blood of animal like horses and cows. I did not know whether such bats could be found in India, but I had certainly read about them in books from abroad. And those did not just talk about bats. They even spoke of bodies of dead men that came out of graves in the middle of the night to drink the blood of people who were asleep. Such creatures were also called vampires. The story of Count Dracula was something I had read in school.

It annoyed me to think that the man had raised the subject of vampires in spite of being aware of my aversion to bats.

We both fell silent.

Then we came to the mango grove and the house could be seen quite clearly. Here he stopped abruptly and said, 'It's been a pleasure meeting you. You're going to stay here for some time, aren't you?'

'About a week.'

'Good. Then we shall certainly meet again. Usually, in the evening,' he said, pointing towards the graveyard, 'I can be found there. My forefathers were buried in the same place. I shall show you their graves tomorrow.'

I said silently to myself, 'The less I see of you the better.' Bat I could not bear to look at, anyway. A discussion on those stupid creatures was even worse. There were plenty of other things to think about.

As I climbed up the steps of the veranda, I turned

back for a moment and saw the man disappear among the mango trees. By that time, the jackals had started their chorus beyond the rice fields.

It was the month of October; yet, it felt hot and oppressive inside the room. I tossed and turned in my bed after dinner. I even toyed with the idea of opening the door of my room which I had closed for fear of the bat flying in again. In the end, I decided against it, not so much because of the bat, but because of something else. If the caretaker was a light sleeper, perhaps there was no danger of being burgled. But what if a stray dog came in through the open door and chewed up my slippers? This could happen easily in a small mofussil town. In fact, I had had that kind of experience more than once. So, instead of opening the door, I opened the window that faced the west. A lovely breeze came wafting in.

I soon fell asleep and began to have a strange dream.

In my dream I saw the same man peering through the window of my room and smiling at me. His eyes were bright green and his teeth sharp and narrow. Then I saw the man take a step back, raise his arms and leap through the window. It seemed almost as though it was the sound of his arrival that woke me.

I opened my eyes and saw that dawn had broken. What an awful dream!

I rose and yelled for a cup of tea. I must finish breakfast and leave early, or I would never get all my work done.

Madhusudam seemed a little preoccupied as he placed my tea on the table in the veranda. I asked, 'What's the matter, Madhusudan? Are you unwell? Or didn't you sleep last night?'

Madhu said, 'No, babu. I am quite all right. It's my calf.'

'What happened to your calf?'

'It died last night. Got bitten by a snake probably.'

'What!'

'Yes, sir. It was only a week old. Something bit its throat—God knows if it was a cobra.'

I began to feel uneasy. Bitten on the throat? Where did I...? Of course. A vampire bat! Wasn't it only yesterday that I was thinking of the same thing? Vampire bats did suck blood from the throats of animals. But, of course, the calf might indeed have been bitten by a snake. That was perfectly possible, especially if the calf happened to be sleeping. Why was I trying to link the death of a calf with vampire bats?

I uttered a few words of comfort to Madhusudan

and returned to my room. My eyes moved towards the ceiling involuntarily.

The bat was back.

It was my mistake. I should not have left the window open. I decided to keep all the doors and windows closed tonight, no matter how stuffy it became.

~

I spent a rather enjoyable day among the old terracotta temples. The workmanship of those who had done the carving on the walls was truly remarkable.

I took a bus from Hetampur and returned to Shiuri at about half past four in the evening.

I had to pass the graveyard in order to get home. The busy day had nearly made me forget the man I had met the day before. The sight of the man, standing under a tree just outside the graveyard, therefore, came as a surprise. Perhaps the best thing would be to pretend not to have seen him and walk on. But that was not to be. Just as I bent my head and increased the speed of my walking, he leapt towards me.

'Did you sleep well last night?'

I said 'Yes' without stopping. But it was clear that, like

yesterday, he would walk with me. He began walking fast to keep pace with me. 'I have a funny habit, you see,' he said. 'I cannot sleep at night. So I sleep tight during the day and from evening to early morning, I roam around here and there. Oh, I cannot explain to you the joy of walking around at night. You have no idea how many different things are simply crying out to be seen, to be heard in this very graveyard! Have you ever thought of these beings that have spent years and years, lying under the ground, stuffed in a wooden box? Have you wondered about their unfulfilled desires? No one wants to stay a prisoner. Each one of them wants to come out! But not many know the secret of getting out. So, in their sadness, some weep, some wail and others sigh. In the middle of the night, when the jackals go to sleep and the crickets become quiet, those who have sensitive ears—like mine— can hear the soft moaning of these people, nailed into a box. But, as I told you, one would have to have very sharp ears. My eyes and ears work very well at night. Just like a bat's.'

I must ask Madhusudan about this man, I thought. There were a few questions I wanted answered, but I knew there would be no point in asking the man. How long had he really spent in Shiuri? What did he do for a living? Where did he live?

He continued to walk beside me and talk incessantly.

'I don't often make the effort to go and meet people,' he said, 'but I simply had to come and meet you. I do hope you won't deprive me of the pleasure of your company for the remainder of your stay.'

This time I could not control myself. I stopped, turned towards the man and said rather rudely, 'Look, mister, I have come only for a week. I have a vast amount of work to do. I don't see how I can possibly spend any time with you.'

The man, at first, seemed a little crestfallen at my words. Then he smiled and said in a tone that sounded mild yet oddly firm, 'You may not give me your company, but surely I can give you mine? Besides, I was not talking about the time when you'd be busy doing your work— during the day, that is.'

There was no need to waste any more time with him. I said namaskar abruptly and strode towards my house.

'Jagdish Mukherjee? I don't think... Oh, wait a minute! Is he short? Wears a jacket and trousers? Is a little dark?'

'Yes, yes.'

'Oh, babu, that man is crazy. Quite mad. In fact, he's only recently been discharged from the asylum. They say he's now cured. How did you come across him? I haven't seen him for ages. His father was a priest called Nilmani Mukherjee. A nice man, but I believe he, too, went quite cuckoo before his death.'

I did not pursue the matter. All I said was, 'That bat had come in again. But it was entirely my fault. I had kept the window open. I hadn't realized some of its grills were broken.'

Madhu said, 'Tomorrow morning I shall have those gaps filled. Perhaps during the night you should keep the window close.'

After dinner, I finished writing notes on the temples I had seen that day. Then I loaded my camera with a new roll. Glancing out of the window, I saw that the clouds of last night had cleared, leaving everything awash in the moonlight.

I went and sat outside on the veranda for a while and returned to my room at around 11 p.m. Then I drank a glass of water and finally went to bed. Jagdish Mukherjee's words were still ringing in my ears. No doubt, in this scientific age, his words were no more than the ravings of a mad man. I must find out which asylum he had gone to and which doctor had treated him.

The clouds having dispersed, the oppressive feeling of the night before had gone. Keeping the window closed was not difficult. In fact, that night I had to use the extra sheet I had brought. I fell asleep soon after closing my eyes. But I woke a little while later, though I could not tell the time nor what it was that had disturbed my sleep. Then I saw a square patch of moonlight on the wall and my heart lurched.

God knew when the window had opened. Light was coming in through the open window. In that patch of light I saw the shadow of something flying in a circle, again and again.

Holding my breath carefully, I turned my head and looked up. This time I could see the bat.

It kept flying in a circle right over my bed, and slowly began to come down.

I mustered all my courage. It would be disastrous if I lost my will power at a moment like this. Without taking my eyes off the bat, I stretched my right hand towards the bedside table and picked up my large, hardbound notebook. Just as the bat made a final swoop, ready to attack my throat, I struck its head with the notebook, using all my strength.

It went shooting out of the window, knocking once against the broken grills, and landed on the ground outside. The next instant, I thought I heard someone running across the ground.

I rushed to the window and peered out. Nothing could be seen. There was no sign of the bat.

I could not go back to sleep after that.

~

The first rays of the sun in the morning wiped out the horrors of the night. There was no reason to assume that the bat was a vampire. Yes, it had certainly come very close to me, but how could it be proved that it had done so with the intention of sucking my blood? If that weird character in the graveyard had not raised the subject of vampires, I would not even have dreamt of it. A bat in Shiuri would have struck me as no different from a bat in Calcutta.

I decided to forget the whole thing. There was some work to be done in Hetampur. I finished my cup of tea and left at around half-past six.

As I approached the graveyard, I came upon a

startling sight. A few local people were carrying Jagdish Mukherjee. He appeared to be unconscious and his forehead had a large, black bruise.

'What happened to him?' I asked.

One of the men laughed.

'Fell down from the tree, probably,' he said.

'What! Why should he fall from a tree? What could he have been doing on a tree top?'

'You don't know, babu. This man is totally mad. He seemed to have made a slight recovery lately. Before that, every evening as soon as it got dark, he used to go and hang upside down from trees. Just like a bat!'

Translated from the Bengali by Gopa Majumdar

the parrot's tale

Rabindranath Tagore

O nce there was a bird. He was uneducated. He sang, but did not read the shastras. He hopped about and flew, but didn't know good manners.

'Such a bird is of no use,' declared the king, 'but he harms the sale of fruit in the royal market by eating up the wild fruits in the forest.'

He sent for the minister. 'Educate this bird,' he ordered.

II

The king's nephews were given the responsibility of educating the bird.

The pundits assembled and considered the matter at length. The question was: 'What is the reason for this creature's lack of education?'

They concluded that there was not much room for learning in the bird's nest, made from a few humble straws and twigs. Hence it was necessary, first of all, to make him a proper cage.

Receiving their dues, the royal pundits went home happily.

III

The goldsmith now set about making a golden cage. So marvellous was the cage he made, people from far-off lands came there to admire it. Some said, 'It is the height of education.' 'Even if he doesn't get an education, at least he has a cage,' declared others. 'What a lucky bird!'

The goldsmith was rewarded with a bagful of money as reward. He went home happily.

The pundits got down to the business of educating the bird. 'This is not a task to be achieved with just a few books,' they declared, inhaling snuff.

Now the royal nephews summoned all the scribes. Copying many textbooks and making copies of copies, they produced a mountain-high pile of books. Anyone who saw it exclaimed: 'Shabash—congratulations! This heap of knowledge is full to bursting!'

Loading a bullock with all the money they received as payment, the scribes rushed home. They no longer had any trouble making both ends meet.

There was no end to the royal nephews' fussing over the very expensive cage. There was no end to all the repair and maintenance, either. And there was such a to-do about dusting, wiping and polishing that the sight made everyone declare: 'These are signs of progress.'

The work required a lot of manpower, and to keep an eye on the workers, even more men had to be deployed. Month by month, they collected their payments by the fistful and stuffed the money in their safes.

These men, and all their maternal and paternal cousins, settled happily in palatial brick-built mansions.

IV

Many other things are lacking in this world, but there is no dearth of fault-finders. 'The cage is improving,' they said, 'but nobody asks after the bird.'

The matter reached the king's ears. He sent for the nephews and demanded: 'O nephews, what's this I hear?'

'Maharaj,' said the nephews, 'if you want to hear

the truth, summon the goldsmiths, pundits, scribes, the maintenance workers and their supervisors. It's because the fault-finders don't get enough to eat that they say such evil things.'

From this reply, the situation became clear to the king. Golden necklaces were ordered at once, to adorn the nephews' necks.

V

The king wanted to see for himself the tremendous pace at which the bird's education was progressing.

At once, the area near the portico began to resound with the noise of conchs, bells, dhak, dhol, kada, nakada, turi, bheri, damama, kanshi, flutes, gongs, khol, cymbals, mridanga and jagajhampa. With full-throated abandon, shaking the unshaven locks of their tikis atop their tonsured heads, the pundits began to chant mantras. The masons, workmen, goldsmiths, scribes, supervisors and their maternal and paternal cousins sang the king's glory.

'Maharaj, can you see what a to-do there is!' observed a nephew.

'Amazing! The noise is quite extraordinary,' observed the Maharaja.

'It's not just the noise; the money that's gone into it is not inconsiderable either,' the nephew pointed out.

Delighted, the Maharaja crossed the portico and was about to mount his elephant when a fault-finder concealed in the bushes called out: 'Maharaj, have you had a look at the bird?'

The king was startled. 'Oh no!' he exclaimed. 'I had clean forgotten. I haven't seen the bird.'

He went back and told the pundit, 'I need to observe your technique for training the bird.'

He was duly shown the technique. What he saw pleased him greatly. The method was so much more important than the bird that the bird could not be seen at all; it seemed needless to see him. The king realized that the arrangements lacked nothing. There was no grain in the cage, no water, just a mass of pages torn from a mass of books, being stuffed down the bird's throat by the end of a quill pen. The bird's song could not be heard of course, for it was too stifled even to scream. It was a thrilling sight, enough to give one goosepimples.

Now, while mounting his elephant, the king instructed the Chief Ear-puller to tweak the fault-finder thoroughly by the ears.

VI

Day by day, the bird arrived at a half-dead state, in a civilized fashion. His guardians saw this as a hopeful sign. But still, by natural instinct, the bird would gaze at the morning light and flutter his wings in a way that was unacceptable. In fact, one day he was seen struggling to cut through the bars of his cage with his fragile beak.

'What audacity!' cried the Kotwal, the law-maker.

Now the blacksmith appeared in the training quarters, armed with bellows, hammer and fire. How hard he beat the iron! Iron shackles were forged, and the bird's wings were clipped.

Gravely shaking their heads, the king's associates declared: 'In this kingdom, the birds lack not only brains, but gratitude as well.'

Now, armed with pen in one hand and rod in the other, the pundits accomplished the dramatic feat called education.

The blacksmiths gained so much importance, their wives bedecked themselves with ornaments, and seeing the alertness of the Kotwal, the king bestowed him with a shiropa, a turban of honour.

VII

The parrot died. Nobody could say when.

The wretched fault-finder spread the word: 'The bird is dead.'

'Nephews, what is this I hear?' demanded the king.

'Maharaj, the bird's training is complete,' declared the nephews.

'Does he hop about any more?' the king enquired.

'Arre Rama! No,' demurred the nephew.

'Does he fly any more?'

'No.'

'Does he sing any more?'

'No.'

'Does he scream if he does not receive grain for his feed?'

'No.'

'Bring the bird to me at once,' the king ordered. 'Let me see him.'

The bird was brought. Along with the bird came the Kotwal, paiks and horsemen.

The king prodded the bird. But the bird neither opened his beak, nor made any sound. Only the dry pages torn from books rustled and sighed in his belly.

Outside, stirred by the fresh spring breeze blowing in from the south, the sighing of new leaves spread anguish in the sky, above the newly blossoming woods.

Translated from the Bengali by Radha Chakravarty

swami and friends

R.K. Narayan

For ten-year-old Swami, life mostly consists of adventures with his friends, avoiding homework and coping as best he can with his teachers and other adults. His greatest passion is the M.C.C.—the Malgudi Cricket Club—which he has founded together with his friends. But the innocent and impulsive Swami lands in trouble when he is carried away by the unrest that takes hold of the country in 1930...

—Editor

$\mathcal{E}$arly next morning as Swaminathan lay in bed watching a dusty beam of sunlight falling a few yards off his bed, his mind, which was just emerging from sleep, became conscious of a vague worry. Swaminathan asked himself what that worry was. It must be something connected with school. Homework? No. Matters were all right in that direction. It was something connected with dress. Bonfire, bonfire of clothes. Yes. It now dawned upon him with an oppressive clearness that he had thrown his cap into the patriotic bonfire of the previous evening; and of course his father knew nothing about it.

What was he going to wear for school today? Telling his father and asking for a new cap was not practicable. He could not go to school bareheaded.

He started for the school in a mood of fatalistic abandon, with only a coat and no cap on. And the fates were certainly kind to him. At least Swaminathan believed that he saw the hand of God in it when he reached the school and found the boys gathered in the road in front of the school in a noisy irregular mob.

Swaminathan passed through the crowd unnoticed till he reached the school gate. A perfect stranger belonging to the Third Form stopped him and asked: 'Where are you going?' Swaminathan hesitated for a moment to discover if there was any trap in this question and said: 'Why—er... Of course...'

'No school today,' declared the stranger with emphasis, and added passionately, 'one of the greatest sons of the

Motherland has been sent to gaol.'

'I won't go to school,' Swaminathan said, greatly relieved at this unexpected solution to his cap problem.

The Head Master and the teachers were standing in the front veranda of the school. The Head Master looked careworn. Ebenezar was swinging his cane and pacing up and down. For once, the boys saw D. Pillai, the History teacher, serious, and gnawing his close-clipped moustache in great agitation. The crowd in the road had become brisker and noisier, and the school looked forlorn. At five minutes to ten the first bell rang, hardly heard by anyone except those standing near the gate. A conference was going on between the teachers and the Head Master. The Head Master's hand trembled as he pulled out his watch and gave orders for the second bell. The bell that at other times gave out a clear rich note now sounded weak and inarticulate. The Head Master and the teacher were seen coming towards the gate, and a lull came upon the mob.

The Head Master appealed to the boys to behave and get back to their classes quietly. The boys stood firm. The teachers, including D. Pillai, tried and failed. After uttering a warning that the punishment to follow would be severe, the Head Master withdrew. Thundering shouts of 'Bharat Mata ki Jai!' 'Gandhi ki Jai!' and 'Gaura Sankar ki Jai!' followed him.

There were gradual unnoticed additions of all sorts of people to the original student mob. Now zestful adult voices could be detected in the frequent cries of 'Gandhi ki Jai!'

Half a dozen persons appointed themselves leaders, and ran about crying: 'Remember, this is a hartal. This is a day of mourning. Observe it in the proper spirit of sorrow and silence.'

Swaminathan was an unobserved atom in the crowd. Another unobserved atom was busily piling up small stones before him, and flinging them with admirable aim at the panes in the front part of the school building. Swaminathan could hardly help following his example. He picked up a handful of stones and searched the building with his eyes. He was disappointed to find at least seventy per cent of the panes already attended to.

He uttered a sharp cry of joy as he discovered a whole ventilator, consisting of small square glasses, in the Head Master's room intact! He sent a stone at it and waited with cocked-up ears for the splintering noise as the stone hit the glass, and the final shivering noise, a fraction of a second later, as the piece crashed on the floor. It was thrilling.

A puny man came running into the crowd announcing excitedly, 'Work is going on in the Board High School.'

This horrible piece of news set the crowd in motion. A movement began towards the Board High School, which was situated at the tail-end of Market Road.

When it reached the Board High School, the self-appointed leaders held up their hands and requested the crowd to remain outside and be peaceful, and entered the school. Within fifteen minutes, trickling in by twos and threes, the crowd was in the school hall.

A spokesman of the crowd said to the Head Master, 'Sir, we are not here to create a disturbance. We only want you to close the school. It is imperative. Our leader is in gaol. Our Motherland is in the throes of war.'

The Head Master, a wizened owl-like man, screamed. 'With whose permission did you enter the building? Kindly go out or I shall send for the police.'

This was received with howling, jeering and hooting. And following it, tables and benches were overturned and broken and windows were smashed. Most of the Board

School boys merged with the crowd. A few, however, stood apart. They were first invited to come out; but when they showed reluctance, they were dragged out.

Swaminathan's part in all this was by no means negligible. It was he who shouted 'We will spit on the police' (though it was drowned in the din), when the Head Master mentioned the police. The mention of the police had sent his blood boiling. What brazenness, what shamelessness, to talk of police—the nefarious agents of the Lancashire thumb-cutters! When the pandemonium started, he was behind no one in destroying the school furniture. With tremendous joy he discovered that there were many glass panes untouched yet. His craving to break them could not be fully satisfied in his own school. He ran round collecting ink-bottles and flung them one by one at every pane that caught his eye. When the Board School boys were dragged out, he felt that he could not do much in that line, most of the boys being as big as himself. On the flash of a bright idea, he wriggled through the crowd and looked for the Infant Standards. There he found little children huddled together and shivering with fright. He charged into this crowd with such ferocity that the children scattered about, stumbling and falling. One unfortunate child who shuffled and moved awkwardly received individual attention. Swaminathan pounced upon him, pulled out his cap, threw it down and stamped on it, swearing all the time. He pushed him and dragged him this way and that and then gave him a blow on the head and left him to his fate.

Having successfully paralysed work in the Board School, the crowd moved on in a procession along Market Road. The air vibrated with the songs and slogans uttered in a hundred keys by a hundred voices. Swaminathan found himself wedged in among a lot of unknown people, in one of the last ranks. The glare from the blanched treeless Market Road was blinding. The white dust stirred up by the procession hung like thin mist in the air and choked him. He could see before him nothing but moving backs and shoulders and occasionally odd parts of some building. His throat was dry with shouting, and he was beginning to feel hungry. He was just pondering whether he could just slip out and go home, when the procession came to a sudden halt. In a minute the rear ranks surged forward to see what the matter was.

The crowd was now in the centre of Market Road, before the fountain in the square. On the other side of the fountain were drawn up about fifty constables armed with *lathis*. About a dozen of them held up the procession. A big man, with a cane in his hand and a revolver slung from his belt, advanced towards the procession. His leather straps and belts and the highly-polished boots and hose made him imposing in Swaminathan's eyes. When he turned his head Swaminathan saw to his horror that it was Rajam's father! Swaminathan could not help feeling sorry that it should be Rajam's father. Rajam's father! Rajam's father to be at the head of those traitors! The Deputy Superintendent of Police fixed his eyes on his wrist-watch and said, 'I declare this assembly unlawful. I give it five minutes to disperse.' At the end of five minutes he looked up and uttered in a hollow voice the word, 'Charge.'

In the confusion that followed Swaminathan was very nearly trampled upon and killed. The policemen rushed into the crowd, pushing and beating everybody. Swaminathan had joined a small group of panic-stricken runners. The policemen came towards them with upraised *lathis*. Swaminathan shrieked to them, 'Don't kill me. I know nothing.' He then heard a series of dull noises as the *lathis* descended on the bodies of his neighbours.

Swaminathan saw blood streaming from the forehead of one. Down came the *lathis* again. Another runner fell down with a groan. On the back of a third the *lathis* fell again and again.

Swaminathan felt giddy with fear. He was running as fast as his legs could carry him. But the policemen kept pace with him; one of them held him up by his hair and asked, 'What business have you here?'

'I don't know anything, leave me, sirs,' Swaminathan pleaded.

'Doing nothing! Mischievous monkey!' said the grim, hideous policeman—how hideous policemen were at close-quarters!—and delivering him a light tap on the head with the *lathi*, ordered him to run before he was kicked.

~

Swaminathan's original intention had been to avoid that day's topic before his father. But as soon as Father came home, even before taking off his coat, he called Mother and gave her a summary of the day's events. He spoke with a good deal of warmth. 'The Deputy Superintendent is a butcher,' he said as he went in to change. Swaminathan was disposed to agree that the Deputy Superintendent was a butcher, as he recollected the picture of Rajam's father looking at his watch, grimly ticking off seconds before giving orders for massacre. Father came out of the dressing-room before undoing his tie, to declare, 'Fifty persons have been taken to the hospital with dangerous contusions. One or two are also believed to be killed.' Turning to Swaminathan he said, 'I heard that schoolboys have given a lot of trouble, what did you do?'

'There was a strike...' replied Swaminathan and discovered here an opportunity to get his cap problem solved. He added, 'Oh, the confusion! You know, somebody pulled off the cap that I was wearing and tore it to bits... I want a cap before I start for school tomorrow.'

'Who was he?' Father asked.

'I don't know, some bully in the crowd.'

'Why did he do it?'

'Because it was foreign...'

'Who said so? I paid two rupees and got it from the Khaddar Stores. It is a black *khaddar* cap. Why do you presume that you know what is what?'

'I didn't do anything. I was very nearly assaulted when I resisted.'

'You should have knocked him down. I bought the cap and the cloth for your coat on the same day in the Khaddar Stores. If any man says that they are not *khaddar*, he must be blind.'

'People say that it was made in Lancashire.'

'Nonsense. You can ask them to mind their business. And if you allow your clothes to be torn by people who think this and that, you will have to go about naked, that is all. And you may also tell them that I won't have a pie of mine sent to foreign countries. I know my duty. Whatever it is, why do not you urchins leave politics alone and mind your business? We have enough troubles in our country without you brats messing up things…'

Swaminathan lay wide awake in bed for a long time. As the hours advanced, and one by one as the lights in the house disappeared, his body compelled him to take stock of the various injuries done to it during the day. His elbows and knees had their own tales to tell: they brought back to his mind the three or four falls that he had had that day. One was—when—yes, when Rajam got down from his car and came to the school, and Swaminathan had wanted to hide himself, and in the hurry stumbled on a heap of stones, and there the knees were badly skinned. And again when the policemen charged, he ran and fell flat before a shop, and some monster ran over him, pinning him with one foot to the ground.

Now as he turned there was a pang about his hips. And then he felt as if a load had been hung from his thighs. And again as he thought of it, he felt a heavy monotonous pain in the head—the merciless rascals! The policeman's *lathi* was none too gentle. And he had been called a monkey! He would—he would see—to call him a monkey! He was no monkey. Only they—the policemen—looked like monkeys, and they behaved like monkeys too.

~

The Head Master entered the class with a slightly flushed face and a hard ominous look in his eyes. Swaminathan wished that he had been anywhere but there at that moment. The Head Master surveyed the class for a few minutes and asked, 'Are you not ashamed to come and sit there after what you did yesterday?' Just as a special honour to them, he read out the names of a dozen or so that had attended the class. After that he read out the names of those that had kept away, and asked them to stand on their benches. He felt that that punishment was not enough and asked them to stand on their desks. Swaminathan was among them and felt humiliated at that eminence. Then they were lectured. When it was over, they were asked to offer explanations one by one. One said that he had had an attack of headache and therefore could not come to the school. He was asked to bring a medical certificate. The second said that while he had been coming to the school on the previous day, someone had told him that there would be no school, and he had gone back home. The Head Master replied that if he was going to listen to every loafer who said there would be no school, he deserved to be flogged. Anyway, why did he not come to the school and verify? No answer. The punishment was pronounced: ten days' attendance cancelled, two rupees fine, and the whole day to be spent on the desk. The third said that he had had an attack of headache. The fourth said that he had had stomach-ache. The fifth said that his grandmother died suddenly just as he was starting for the school. The Head Master asked him if he could bring a letter from his father. No. He had no father. Then who was his guardian? His grandmother. But the grandmother was dead, was she not? No. It was another grandmother. The Head Master asked how many grandmothers a person could have. No answer. Could he bring a letter from his neighbours? No, he could not. None of his neighbours could read or write, because he lived in the more illiterate parts of Ellaman Street. Then the Head Master offered to send a teacher to this illiterate locality to ascertain from the boy's neighbours if the death of the grandmother was a fact. A pause, some perspiration, and then the answer that the neighbours could not possibly know anything about it, since the grandmother died in the village. The Head Master hit him on the knuckles with his cane, called him a street dog, and pronounced the punishment: fifteen days' suspension.

When Swaminathan's turn came, he looked around helplessly. Rajam sat on the third bench in front, and resolutely looked away. He was gazing at the blackboard intently. Yet the back of his head and the pink ears were visible to Swaminathan. It was an intolerable sight. Swaminathan was in acute suspense lest that head should turn and fix its eyes on his; he felt that he would drop from the desk to the floor, if that happened. The pink ears three benches off made him incapable of speech. If only somebody would put a blackboard between his eyes and those pink ears!

He was deaf to the question that the Head Master was putting to him. A rap on his body from the Head Master's cane brought him to himself.

'Why did you keep away yesterday?' asked the Head Master, looking up. Swaminathan's first impulse was to protest that he had never been absent. But the attendance register was there. 'No—no—I was stoned. I tried to come, but they took away my cap and burnt it. Many strong men held me down when I tried to come...When a great man is sent to gaol...I am surprised to see you a slave of the Englishmen...Didn't they cut off—Dacca Muslin— Slaves of slaves...' These were some of the disjointed explanations which streamed into his head, and, which, even at that moment, he was discreet enough not to express. He had wanted to mention a headache, but he found to his distress that others beside him had had one. The Head Master shouted, 'Won't you open your mouth?' He brought the cane sharply down on Swaminathan's right shoulder. Swaminathan kept staring at the Head Master with tearful eyes, massaging with his left hand the spot where the cane was laid. 'I will kill you if you keep on staring without answering my question,' cried the Head Master.

'I—I—couldn't come,' stammered Swaminathan.

'Is that so?' asked the Head Master, and turning to a boy said, 'Bring the peon.'

Swaminathan thought: 'What, is he going to ask the peon to thrash me? If he does any such thing, I will bite everybody dead.' The peon came. The Head Master said to him, 'Now say what you know about this rascal on the desk.'

The peon eyed Swaminathan with a sinister look, grunted, and demanded, 'Didn't I see you break the panes?'

'Of the ventilators in my room?' added the Head Master with zest.

Here there was no chance of escape. Swaminathan kept staring foolishly till he received another whack on the back. The Head Master demanded what the young brigand had to say about it. The brigand had nothing to say. It was a fact that he had broken the panes. They had seen it. There was nothing more to it. He had unconsciously become defiant and did not care to deny the charge. When another whack came on his back, he ejaculated, 'Don't beat me, sir. It pains.' This was an invitation to the Head Master to bring down the cane four times again. He said, 'Keep standing here, on this desk, staring like an idiot, till I announce your dismissal.'

Every pore in Swaminathan's body burnt with the touch of the cane. He had a sudden flood of courage, the courage that comes of desperation. He restrained the tears that were threatening to rush out, jumped down, and, grasping his books, rushed out muttering, 'I don't care for your dirty school.'

how I taught my grandmother to read

Sudha Murty

When I was a girl of about twelve, I used to stay in a village in north Karnataka with my grandparents. Those days, the transport system was not very good, so we used to get the morning paper only in the afternoon. The weekly magazine used to come one day late. All of us would wait eagerly for the bus, which used to come with the papers, weekly magazines and the post.

At that time, Triveni was a very popular writer in the Kannada language. She was a wonderful writer. Her style was easy to read and very convincing. Her stories usually dealt with complex psychological problems in the lives of ordinary people and were always very interesting. Unfortunately for Kannada literature, she died young. Even now, after forty years, people continue to appreciate her novels.

One of her novels, called *Kashi Yatre*, was appearing as a serial in the Kannada weekly *Karmaveera* then. It is the story of an old lady and her ardent desire to go to Kashi or Varanasi. Most Hindus believe that going to Kashi and worshipping Lord Vishweshvara is the ultimate *punya*. This old lady also believed in this, and her struggle to go there was described in that novel. In the story there was also a young orphan girl who falls in love but there was no money for the wedding. In the end, the old lady gives away all her savings without going to Kashi. She says, 'The happiness of this orphan girl is more important than worshipping Lord Vishweshwara at Kashi.'

My grandmother, Krishtakka, never went to school, so she could not read. Every Wednesday the magazine would come and I would read the next episode of this story to her. During that time she would forget all her work and listen with the greatest concentration. Later, she could repeat the entire text by heart. My grandmother too never went to Kashi, and she identified with the novel's protagonist. So, more than anybody else, she was the one most interested in knowing what happened next in the story and used to insist that I read the serial out to her.

After hearing what happened next in *Kashi Yatre,* she would join her friends at the temple courtyard where we children would also gather to play hide and seek. She would discuss the latest episode with her friends. At that time, I never understood why there was so much of debate about the story.

Once I went for a wedding with my cousins to the neighbouring village. In those days, a wedding was a great event. We children enjoyed ourselves thoroughly. We would eat and play endlessly, savouring the freedom because all the elders were busy. I went for a couple of days but ended up staying there for a week.

When I came back to my village, I saw my grandmother in tears. I was surprised, for I had never seen her cry even in the most difficult situations. What had happened? I was worried.

'Avva, is everything all right? Are you okay?'

I used to call her Avva, which means mother in the Kannada spoken in north Karnataka.

She nodded but did not reply. I did not understand and

forgot about it. That night, after dinner, we were sleeping in the open terrace of the house. It was a summer night and there was a full moon. Avva came and sat next to me. She touched my forehead affectionately. I realized she wanted to say something to me. I asked her, 'What is the matter?'

'When I was a young girl I lost my mother,' she said. 'There was nobody to look after me and guide me. My father was a busy man and got married again. In those days people did not consider education to be essential for girls, so I never went to school. I got married very young and had children. I became very busy. Later I had grandchildren and always felt so much happiness in cooking and feeding all of you. At times I used to regret not going to school, so I made sure that my children and grandchildren studied well...'

I could not understand why my sixty-two-year-old grandmother was telling me, a twelve-year-old, the story of her life in the middle of the night. But I knew I loved her immensely and there had to be some reason why she was talking to me. I looked at her face. It was unhappy and her eyes were filled with tears. She was a good-looking lady who was usually always smiling. Even today I cannot forget the worried expression on her face.

I leaned forward and held her hand.

'Avva, don't cry. What is the matter? Can I help you in any way?'

'Yes, I need your help. You know when you were away, *Karmaveera* came as usual. I opened the magazine. I saw the picture that accompanies the story of *Kashi Yatre* but I could not understand anything that was written. Many times I rubbed my hands over the pages wishing they could understand what was written. But I knew it was not possible. If only I was educated enough. I waited eagerly for you to return. I felt you would come early and read for me. I even thought of going to the village and asking you to read for me. I could have asked somebody in this village but I was too embarrassed to do so. I felt so very dependent and helpless. We are well-off, but what use is money when I cannot be independent?'

I did not know what to answer. Avva continued.

'I have decided I want to learn the Kannada alphabets from tomorrow onwards. I will work very hard. I will keep Saraswati Pooja day as the deadline. That day I should be able to read a novel on my own. I want to be independent.'

I saw the determination on her face. Yet I laughed at her.

'Avva, at this age of sixty-two you want to learn the alphabets? All your hair is grey, your hands are wrinkled, you wear spectacles and you work so much in the kitchen...'

Childishly I made fun of the old lady. But she just smiled.

'For a good cause if you are determined, you can overcome any obstacle. I will work harder than anybody but I will do it. For learning there is no age bar.'

The next day onwards I started my tuition. Avva was a wonderful student. The amount of homework she did was amazing. She would read, repeat, write and recite. I was her teacher and she was my first student. Little did I know then that one day I would become a teacher in Computer Science and teach hundreds of students.

The Dassara festival came as usual. Secretly I bought *Kashi Yatre* which had been published as a novel by that time. My grandmother called me to the puja place and made me sit down on a stool. She gave me a gift of a frock material. Then she did something unusual. She bent down and touched my feet. I was surprised and taken aback. Elders never touch the feet of youngsters. We always touched the feet of God, elders and teachers. We consider that as a mark of respect. It is a great tradition but today the reverse had happened. It was not correct.

She said, 'I am touching the feet of a teacher, not my granddaughter; a teacher who taught me so well, with so much affection that I can read any novel confidently in such a short period. Now I am independent. It is my duty to respect a teacher. Is it not written in our scriptures that a teacher should be respected, irrespective of the gender and age?'

I did return namaskara to her by touching her feet and gave my gift to my first student. She opened it and read immediately the title *Kashi Yatre* by Triveni and the publisher's name.

I knew then that my student had passed with flying colours.

mister owl and missus

Sukumar Ray

Mister says to Missus Owl,
>> I just love it when you howl,
Listening absent-mindedly
>> My soul dances blindedly!
That rubbed voice and scrubbed croon
>> That upswelling happy swoon!
Just one of your ear-splitting hoots
>> Rips the trees out of their roots,
A twist, a turn in every note
>> Crescendos creaking from that throat!
All my fears all my woes
>> All my throbby sobby lows,
Are all forgotten thanks to you
>> My darling singing Owleroo,

Moonbright beauty, sweet as sleep,
    Your nightly songs, they make me weep.

Translated by Sampurna Chattarji from
the Bengali original 'Payncha aar Paynchani'

pumpkin-grumpkin

(If) Pumpkin-Grumpkin dances—
Don't for heaven's sake go where the stable horse
                                                prances;
Don't look left, don't look right, don't take no silly
                                                chances.
Instead cling with all four legs to the holler-radish
                                                branches.

(If) Pumpkin-Grumpkin cries—
Beware! Beware! Don't sit on rooftops high up in
                                                the skies;
Crouch down low on a machan bundled to the eyes,

Sing 'Radhe Krishno Radhe' till your lusty throat
dries.

(If) Pumpkin-Grumpkin laughs—
Stand next to the kitchen poised on straight and
skinny calves;
Speak Persian in a misty voice and breathe through
silken scarves;
Sleep on the grass, skip all three meals, no doing
things by halves!

(If) Pumpkin-Grumpkin runs—
Make sure you scramble up the windows all at once;
Mix rouge with hookah water and on your face smear
tons;
And don't dare look up at the sky, thinking you're
great guns!

(If) Pumpkin-Grumpkin calls—
Clap legal hats on to your heads, float in basins down
the halls;
Pound spinach into healing paste and smear your
forehead walls;

And with a red-hot pumice-stone rub your nose until
it crawls.

Those of you who find this foolish and dare to laugh
it off,
When Pumpkin-Grumpkin gets to know you won't
want to scoff.
Then you'll see which words of mine are full of truth,
and how,
Don't come running to me *then,* I'm telling you right
now.

*Translated by Sampurna Chattarji from
the Bengali original 'Kumro Potaash'*

big brother

Premchand

$\mathcal{M}$y brother was five years older than me, but only three classes ahead. He started studying at the same age as I did but he didn't want to hurry in an important matter such as education. He wanted to build on a strong foundation. So he took two years to do what could be done in one year. If the foundation was not strong how could a building be built to last?

I was younger. I was nine; he was fourteen. To check me and keep an eye on me was his birthright. And decency said that I must follow his command as if it was the Law.

He was studious by nature. He always sat with an open book in front of him. Sometimes, to rest his brain, he would draw pictures of birds, dogs or cats on the margins of his books and notebooks. Sometimes, he would write the same name or word or sentence over and over again. Sometimes, he would write a line of poetry in a beautiful handwriting. Sometimes, he would write things that had neither meaning nor sense. Once, I saw the following written in his copy: Special, Ameena, Brothers-Brothers, Actually, Brother-Brother, Radheshyam, Mr Radheshyam, For One Hour. And after this he had made the drawing of a man. I tried my best to make sense of this riddle but I couldn't. I didn't have the courage to ask him. After all, he was in the ninth standard; I in the fifth. How could I dare to make sense of his writings!

I was not at all interested in studying. Sitting with a book for even one hour made me restless. The first chance I got, I would run away from the hostel and go to the playground and sometimes play with marbles, sometimes fly paper butterflies, and my day would be made if a friend showed up. We would climb up on the roof and take turns jumping off, or swing on the gate and pretend it was a motorcar. But the moment I entered the room and saw Big Brother, or Big B's angry face, I would get scared to death. His first question would be: 'Where were you?' The question was always asked in the same tone and my answer was always silence. I don't know why I could never say I had gone out to play. My silence would say that I accept my crime and Big B would have no other option but to greet me with the following words that showed both his love and anger:

'If you continue to study English like this, you can go on trying for the rest of your life and you still won't learn one word. Studying the English language is not a joke; everyone can't master it. Or else every Tom, Dick and Harry would be a master of English. You have to toil day and night to learn it, and you can never fully learn it either. All sorts of learned men can't actually write, let alone speak in English. And you are such an idiot that you don't learn from my example. You can see for yourself how hard I work. And if you can't see, you are blind and stupid. Every day there is a play or a festival. Have you ever seen me go for even one of them? Every day there is a hockey or cricket match. I never go anywhere near them. I am always studying, yet I end up studying in the same class for two, sometimes even three years. Then, how do you expect to pass despite wasting all your time in fun and games? Do you want to spend the rest of your life in the same class? If this is the way you want to waste your life, you might as well go back home and play gulli-danda. Why are you wasting our poor father's hard-earned money?'

I would listen to this lecture and start crying. I had no answer. I was guilty as charged. Big B was an old hand at giving lectures. He could say such hard-hitting things, aim such barbed arrows that my heart would break into pieces and my confidence would shatter. Yet I didn't have the strength for such do-or-die labour. At such times of despair, I would think, 'Maybe it is best to go back home. Why should I take on something that is beyond my abilities and destroy my life? I am willing to stay illiterate.' But the very thought of so much hard work made my head spin. In an hour or two, the clouds of despair would part and I would decide to study hard. I would make a timetable. After all, how could I begin work without first drawing up a scheme or a plan? There was no room for games and sports in this timetable. According to this plan, I would get up at six a.m., wash, eat my breakfast and sit down to study. From six to eight, it was English; eight to nine Maths; nine to nine-thirty History; then eat my mid-day meal and go off to school. I would return from school at half-past three, rest for half an hour, then study Geography from four to five, Grammar from five to six, stroll for half an hour in front of the hostel; English composition from six-thirty to seven; translation from eight to nine after dinner; Hindi from nine to ten; different subjects from ten to eleven; and then go to bed.

But it is one thing to make a timetable, another to follow it. I would break the rules from the very first day. The greenery of the sports field, the sweet breeze that blew there, the joy of running after the football, the pick-and-throw of kabaddi, the speed and sureness of volleyball—all these would pull me in strange and unknown ways. Once on the sports field, I would forget everything else. That murderous timetable, those books that would blind me one day—I would remember nothing. And Big B would get yet another occasion to give his lecture. I began to run from the very sight of him. I would try my best to stay away from his all-seeing eyes. I would enter the room on tiptoe lest he spotted me. The moment he looked in my direction, I could feel my life ebbing out of me. I constantly felt as though a sword dangled above my head. But just as man remains caught up in the affairs of the world even at a time of trouble or death, my interest in fun and games remained unabated despite the scoldings and insults.

II

The yearly exams took place. Big B failed, I not only passed but also stood first in my class. There was now only a difference of two classes between him and me. There was a lot I wanted to tell Big B: 'What happened to all your hard work? Look at me; I had a lot of fun playing and yet I have stood first in my class.'

But he was so sad that I felt truly sorry for him and the thought of sprinkling salt on his wounds seemed a shameful thing to do. My self-confidence, however, grew—as did my pride. And with it Big B's awe lessened. I began to take part in fun and games with a greater sense of freedom. I had decided: if he ever tries to give me a lecture I shall tell him what I think. I shall say, 'What have you gained after all the long hours of labour? Look at me, I played all day and yet I stood first in my class!' Though I didn't have the courage to actually say these words aloud, it was clear from my behaviour that Big B's days of tyrannical rule over me were a thing of the past.

Big B sensed it. He was quite clever in these simple

matters. One day, when after playing gulli-danda all morning, I was returning home in time for my meal, Big B was ready and waiting to attack. He pounced on me, 'I can see that passing this year and coming first in your class has gone to your head. But, my dear brother, remember that many great men have lost their pride; you are nothing in comparison to them. You must have read about Ravan's fate. What have you learnt from reading about him? Or did you just read without understanding? Simply passing in History is not enough; the real thing is the growth and development of your brain. You must understand whatever you read. Ravan ruled over a large empire. Such kings are called chakravarti kings, or supreme rulers. The English too rule over large parts of the world but they cannot be called chakravarti. Many countries do not accept the supremacy of the English; they remain independent and free. But Ravan was a chakravarti ruler. All other rulers paid him a tax. Even the gods obeyed him. Even the gods of fire and water accepted him as their master. Yet what was Ravan's end? Pride caused him to fall. In the end, there was no one with him. A man may do any wrong but he must not be proud. The day you become proud, your days are numbered.

'You must have read about Satan. He began to believe that there could be no greater believer in God than him. In the end he was pushed out from Heaven and thrown into Hell. The Emperor of Rome too became a victim of pride. He died a beggar. You have merely passed one class and it has gone to your head. Remember, you have not passed because of hard work; it is simply good luck, a matter of chance. But it won't happen every time. In gulli-danda sometimes you get a blind shot; it doesn't make you an expert player. The expert player is one whose shots never go waste. Don't go by the fact that I have failed. When you come to my class you will know how tough it is. When you have to read Algebra and Geometry, the History of England, and remember the names of the kings, all eight Henrys! Do you think it is easy to remember which event took place during which King Henry's rule? If you write Henry VIII instead of Henry VII you lose all your marks. Not even a zero; you get nothing! What do you know about anything? There were dozens of James, another dozen Williams and thousands of Charles. It is enough to make your head spin. They couldn't even think of new names; instead, they kept adding II, IV, V after the same name. I could have told them a million names, had someone asked me.

'And Geometry...only God can save you from it! If, instead of a b c, you write a c b you end up losing all your marks. No one ever asks these cruel examiners what is the difference between a b c and a c b? Why do they kill innocent students over pointless, silly things? Whether you eat rice, dal and roti or dal, rice and roti—what is the difference? But do these examiners care? They want students to memorize every word that is written in the textbooks. And this learning by rote they have called Education. But what is the use of memorizing these pointless things? If you drop that perpendicular over this line, then the base will be double the first line. Ask them what is the advantage or purpose. Whether it is double or half—how does it benefit me? But if you want to pass in the exams you have to remember all these nonsensical details.

'Or they say—write an essay on Punctuality in two-three pages. You open your copy, pen in hand, lost in thought. Everyone knows that it is good to be punctual, it brings order and discipline in a person's life, people like a punctual person, it is good for business. But how can you write four pages on this? What is the point of taking four pages to write on something that can be said in one line? I call this stupidity. This is wasting time, not saving it. I think people should say what they have to say as briefly as possible and then get going. But, no, you have to cover four pages with ink, no matter how you do it. What is this if it isn't cruelty towards students? And to top it all, they say "Write in brief"! Write on Punctuality but take four pages! Wonderful! It is like telling someone to run fast slowly! Does it make any sense? Even a child knows it is silly but not these teachers. They think they are know-alls. You will know how tough it is when you come to my class. You are flying high these days because you have stood first in your class. But you must listen to me. I may have failed but I am older than you. I have more experience of the world than you have. Listen carefully to what I have to say, or else you will regret.'

Fortunately, it was time to go to school or no one knows when that lecture would have ended. My meal seemed tasteless. If I am insulted like this after passing, I wondered, what would be my fate if I fail? I was terrified of the scary picture Big B had painted of the sheer amount of work that had to be done in his class. It is a wonder that I didn't run away from school after that lecture. But despite all the insults that had been heaped upon me, my disinterest in books remained as before. I never allowed any opportunity to play to slip from my hands. I would read, but very little—just enough to complete the work given to me and save me from the teachers' scoldings. The confidence I had gained soon disappeared and I went back to living like a guilty thief.

III

The yearly examinations came around once again and it so happened that I passed once again and Big B failed yet again. I hadn't worked very hard but I don't know how I stood first in my class. I myself was amazed. Big B had tried his level best. He had memorized every word of the syllabus. He would study till ten in the night and then again from four in the morning and from six till nine before leaving for school. Yet he failed. I pitied him. When the results were announced, he burst into tears. My own joy was dimmed. If I had failed too Big B would have been less unhappy but who can undo the doings of Fate.

Now only one class separated Big B and me. An unkind thought arose in my mind: If Big B were to fail yet again, he and I would be in the same class. How would he, then, scold me? But with a great deal of effort I removed the wicked thought. After all, Big B scolded me for my own good. While I hated his lectures when he was delivering them, I knew it was because of his constant preaching that I cleared one class after another, and that too with such good marks.

By now Big B had softened a great deal. Several times, despite finding ample opportunities to scold me, he would hold on to his patience. Perhaps he had realized that he no longer had the right to scold me, or if he had the right then it was much reduced. My wilfulness increased. I began to take unfair advantage of his patience. I began to believe that I would pass—whether I studied or not—because Fate was with me. And so, the little studying I used to do because of Big B's terror stopped. My newest hobby was kite-flying and my entire day would pass in pursuing it. But I still respected Big B. So I would go off to fly kites when he wasn't looking. The various issues relating to kite-flying—how to tie knots expertly, how to cut the strings of competitors' kites, how to enter kite-flying competitions—were dealt with secretly. I didn't want Big B to think that my respect for him had lessened in any way.

One day, close to evening, I was far away from the hostel, running madly after a cut kite. My eyes were glued to the sky and my heart was set on that traveller from the skies that was slowly heading towards the ground as though a heavenly spirit was disinterestedly about to enter a new body. An army of boys, armed with long poles and thorny twigs, was running to catch it. No one was concerned about anything else except the trailing kite. It was almost as though all of us were flying with the kite through the skies where there were no cars, no trams, no lorries.

Suddenly, I ran into Big B who was perhaps returning from the market. He caught my hand there and then and spoke angrily, 'Aren't you ashamed of yourself—running around with these urchins after a worthless kite? Have you no sense? Don't you know you are no longer in a lower class? You are now in the Eighth Standard, just one class behind me. You must give some thought to your position in life. There was a time when people passed the Eighth Standard and became Deputy Tehsildars. I know so many Middle School Pass who have risen to become top-class Deputy Magistrates and Superintendents. So many of our country's leaders and newspaper editors have passed only the Eighth Standard. Some of the most learned men work under them whereas you—you who are studying in the same Eighth Standard—go running around after kites with a bunch of street urchins! I feel saddened by your thoughtlessness.

'You are intelligent, there is no doubt about it, but what good is intelligence if it destroys our pride in ourselves? You must be thinking—I am only one class behind my elder brother and so he doesn't have the right to say anything to me any more. But you are wrong. I am five years older than you. Even if you and I are studying in the same class—and if I continue to get the same results I shall, no doubt, end up in the same class as you and maybe next year you will leave me to go into the next class—the five-year difference between us shall always remain. Not you, not even God, can remove that difference.

'I am five years older than you and shall always remain so. You can never match the experience I have of life and of this world—not even if you do an MA or a DPhil. and a DLitt. You don't get a sense of right and wrong from books alone; you get it from seeing and understanding the world. Our mother has never studied in any class and our father hasn't studied beyond the Fifth or Sixth Standard. You and I can study everything there is to study in the entire world, but our parents will always have the right to scold and correct us. Not because they have given birth to us, but because they have far more experience of the world and shall always have more experience than us. What sort of government does America have, or how many times did Henry VIII marry, or how many planets are there in the universe—they may not know these things, but there are thousands of other things they know that you and I do not.

'God forbid, if I were to fall ill today, wouldn't you panic? You would be able to do nothing except send a telegram to our father. But if our father were here instead of you, he wouldn't send any telegram to anybody; he would neither worry nor panic. He will first try to understand the ailment and cure it as best as he can; if he doesn't succeed he will send for a doctor. Forget falling ill, you and I don't even know how one month's expenses should be made to last the entire month. Whatever our father sends us each month gets finished by the 20th or the 22nd and we are left with nothing. Our breakfast is stopped. We have to evade the washerman and the barber.

Whereas our father has spent less than half of what we spend in a month for the bulk of his life. Not only has he lived well and with dignity but he has supported a large family which includes nine dependents.

'Look at our Headmaster...He has done an MA and that too not from here but from Oxford. He gets a thousand rupees, but who runs his home? His elderly mother! His degree is of no use in this field. He used to run his household on his own earlier but the money would always run short. He was always in debt. Ever since his mother has taken over the reins, it is as though Goddess Lakshmi has entered their home. So, my dear brother, you must get rid of this pride that you have come closer to my class and are, therefore, free to do as you wish. I can'—(raises his hand as if to slap)—'use this too. You hate my words right now, don't you?'

In the face of this new argument, I lowered my head with humility. In front of Big B I felt truly small. Real respect for him swelled in my heart. I spoke with wet eyes, 'No, not at all. Every word you say is true and you have every right to say it.'

Big B clasped me to his bosom and said, 'I don't forbid you from flying kites. I too sometimes feel like flying one, but what can I do? If I go astray, how can I protect you? After all, that duty rests on my head.'

By chance, at that very moment, a kite trailed over our heads. Its cut string dangled behind. A bunch of boys was running to catch it. Big B was tall; he jumped and caught hold of the string and began to run madly towards the hostel. I ran after him.

Translated from the Hindi by Rakhshanda Jalil

rain-making

Shankar

It was evening after a heavy rain. Grandfather was picking flowers from the jasmine bush under a sandalwood tree. The leaves of the tree were full of raindrops. I knew I could make rain if I shook the tree, and Grandfather and I would get a good shower. I liked bathing in the rain. Grandfather might not like it. But it would be great fun.

So I quietly went near the sandalwood tree and shook it with all my strength. There was a heavy shower and both Grandfather and I were soaked. I loved it. But Grandfather did not. He turned on me with an angry look. I was sure he would catch me and beat me. So I ran. He ran after me. I ran fast. But he ran faster. He had almost caught me when he stumbled and fell. I ran away to the paddy fields and hid myself there. I heard Grandfather shout that he would teach me a lesson when I came back home.

I did not want to go home because I feared Grandfather would beat me. I stayed on in the fields. It was getting dark. I was afraid to stay there alone in the darkness. I remembered all the ghost stories I had heard. I stood up, looked around and then ran towards home.

I was still afraid to face Grandfather. So I did not go into the house. I went to the cowshed and took shelter in the loft. From there I could see Grandfather sitting on the veranda saying his prayers.

Grandmother was waiting for me. When I did not turn up she looked for me everywhere in the house. Then she came out and called aloud for me, thinking that I was somewhere in the garden. She could not get any answer. Then she went to Grandfather and asked where I was. 'You look for him in the house,' Grandfather said, 'he is hiding somewhere.'

'He is not in the house,' Grandmother said. 'I looked for him everywhere.'

Then Grandfather stood up and went outside and called aloud, 'Come, Raja, come. I won't beat you.'

But I did not answer him, for I thought that he would beat me.

Grandmother was angry and said, 'He won't come. You drove him away. I heard you say that you would beat him if he came home. Poor child, he is afraid of you and has run away.'

Grandfather called the servants and asked them to go out and look for me. They went out but after a while returned to say that they could not find me. Grandmother started weeping. Grandfather started walking up and down the courtyard.

The news that I was missing spread. Our neighbours came first, then our relatives and then others who had heard the bad news. Many came to offer their sympathies to Grandmother.

Grandfather did not like this. He shouted, 'Nothing has happened to the boy. He is hiding somewhere. Can't some of you go out and find him instead of wasting your time here?'

Some of them went out to search for me.

More and more people came and soon there was a crowd. By now Grandmother had lost all hope of seeing me again. She started telling the people what a good boy I was.

The search parties returned without finding me. Grandmother started weeping loudly. The women in the crowd also wept. The servants of the house joined in the wailing. They all acted as if I were dead.

I felt very sorry for Grandmother. I wanted to come out.

Grandfather was a man of strong will. But I knew that he too felt very sad. He did not, however, lose hope. He stood up, turned in the direction of our family temple and prayed: 'Help me God,' he said. 'Give me my child. I want him now. I cannot wait.' He then stood silent in prayer.

At that moment Uncle returned. He learnt what was happening at home. He looked around and guessed where I was. He came to the cowshed and asked me to come down. I came down. Uncle took me into the house.

Grandfather had just finished his prayer. As he opened his eyes he saw me standing before him. He took me up in his arms in joy, hugged me and said, 'God heard my prayers and has given you back to us.'

—An extract from *Life with Grandfather*

here comes mr oliver

Ruskin Bond

Apart from being our Scoutmaster, Mr Oliver was also our Maths teacher, a subject in which I had some difficulty in obtaining pass marks. Sometimes I scraped through, usually I got something like twenty or thirty out of a hundred.

'Failed again, Bond,' Mr Oliver would say. 'What will you do when you grow up?'

'Become a Scoutmaster, sir.'

'Scoutmasters don't get paid. It's an honorary job. But you could become a cook. That would suit you.'

He hadn't forgotten our Scout camp, when I had been the camp's cook. If Mr Oliver was in a good mood, he'd give me grace marks, passing me by a mark or two. He wasn't a hard man, but he seldom smiled. He was very dark, thin, stooped (from a distance he looked like a question mark), and balding. He was about forty, still a bachelor, and it was said that he had been unlucky in love—that the girl he was going to marry had jilted him at the last moment, had run away with a sailor while he was waiting at the church, ready for the wedding ceremony.

No wonder he always had such a sorrowful look. Mr Oliver did have one inseparable companion—a Dachshund, a snappy little 'sausage' of a dog, who looked upon the human race and especially small boys with a certain disdain and frequent hostility. We called him Hitler. He was impervious to overtures of friendship, and if you tried to pat or stroke him, he would do his best to bite your fingers—or your shin or ankle. However, he was devoted to Mr Oliver and followed him everywhere, except into the classroom; this our Headmaster would not allow. You remember that old nursery rhyme:

Mary had a little lamb,
Its fleece was white as snow,
And everywhere that Mary went
The lamb was sure to go.
Well, we made up our own version of the rhyme, and

I must confess to having had a hand in its composition. It went like this:

Olly had a little dog,
'twas never out of sight,
And everyone that Olly met
The dog was sure to bite!

It followed him about the school grounds. It followed him when he took a walk through the pines, to the Brockhurst tennis courts. It followed him into town and home again. Mr Oliver had no other friend, no other companion. The dog slept at the foot of Mr Oliver's bed. It did not sit at the breakfast table, but it had buttered toast for breakfast and soup and crackers for dinner. Mr Oliver had to take his lunch in the dining-hall with the staff and boys, but he had an arrangement with one of the bearers whereby a plate of dal, rice and chapattis made its way to Mr Oliver's quarters and his well-fed pet.

And then tragedy struck.

Mr Oliver and Hitler were returning to school after their evening walk through the pines. It was dusk, and the light was fading fast. Out of the shadows of the trees emerged a lean and hungry panther. It pounced on the hapless dog, flung it across the road, seized it between its powerful jaws, and made off with its victim into the darkness of the forest.

Mr Oliver, untouched, was frozen into immobility for at least a minute. Then he began calling for help. Some bystanders who had witnessed the incident began shouting, too. Mr Oliver ran into the forest, but there was no sign of dog or panther.

Mr Oliver appeared to be a broken man. He went about his duties with a poker face, but we could all tell that he was grieving for his lost companion. In the classroom he was listless, indifferent to whether or not we followed his calculations on the blackboard. In times of personal loss, the Highest Common Factor made no sense.

Mr Oliver was not to be seen on his evening walk. He stayed in his room, playing cards with himself. He played with his food, pushing most of it aside; there were no chapattis to send home.

'Olly needs another pet,' said Bimal, wise in the ways of adults.

'Or a wife,' said Tata, who thought on those lines.

'He's too old. Over forty. A pet is best,' I said. 'What about a parrot?'

'You can't take a parrot for a walk,' said Bimal. 'Olly

wants someone to walk beside him.'

'A cat, maybe...'

'Hitler hated cats. A cat would be an insult to Hitler's memory.'

'He needs another Dachshund. But there aren't any around here.'

'Any dog will do. We'll ask Chippu to get us a pup.'

Chippu ran the tuck-shop. He lived in the Chotta Simla bazaar, and occasionally we would ask him to bring us tops or marbles or comics or little things that we couldn't get in school. Five of us Boy Scouts contributed a rupee each, and we gave Chippu five rupees and asked him to get us a pup. 'A good breed,' we told him. 'Not a mongrel.'

The next evening Chippu turned up with a pup that seemed to be a combination of at least five different breeds—all good ones, no doubt. One ear lay flat, the other stood upright. It was spotted like a Dalmatian, but it had the legs of a Spaniel and the tail of a Pomeranian. It was quite fluffy and playful, and the tail wagged a lot, which was more than Hitler's ever did.

'It's quite pretty,' said Tata. 'Must be a female.'

'He may not want a female,' said Bimal.

'Let's give it a try,' I said.

During our play hour, before the bell rang for supper, we left the pup on the steps outside Mr Oliver's front door. Then we knocked, and sped into the hibiscus bushes that lined the pathway. Mr Oliver opened the door. He looked down at the pup with an expressionless face. The pup began to paw at Mr Oliver's shoes, loosening one of his laces in the process.

'Away with you!' muttered Mr Oliver. 'Buzz off!' And he pushed the pup away, gently but firmly.

After a break of ten minutes we tried again, but the result was much the same. We now had a playful pup on our hands, and Chippu had gone home for the night. We would have to conceal it in the dormitory.

At first we hid it in Bimal's locker, but it began yapping and struggling to get out. Tata took it into the shower room, but it wouldn't stay there either. It began running around the dormitory, playing with socks, shoes, slippers, and anything else it could get hold of.

'Watch out!' hissed one of the boys. 'Here's Ma Fisher!' Mrs Fisher, the Headmaster's wife, was on her nightly rounds, checking to make sure we were all in bed and not up to some nocturnal mischief.

I grabbed the pup and hid it under my blankets. It was quiet there, happy to nibble at my toes. When Ma Fisher had gone, I let the pup loose again, and for the rest of the night it had the freedom of the dormitory.

At the crack of dawn, before first light, Bimal and I sped out of the dormitory in our pyjamas, taking the pup with us. We banged hard on Mr Oliver's door, and kept knocking until we heard footsteps approaching. As soon as the door opened just a bit (for Mr Oliver, being a cautious man, did not open it all at once) we pushed the pup inside and ran for our lives.

Mr Oliver came to class as usual, but there was no pup with him. Three or four days passed, and still no sign of the pup! Had he passed it on to someone else, or simply let it wander off on its own?

'Here comes Olly!' called Bimal, from our vantage point near the school bell. Mr Oliver was setting out for his evening walk. He was carrying a stout walnut-wood walking stick—to keep panthers at bay, no doubt. He looked neither left nor right, and if he noticed us watching him, he gave no sign of it. But then, scurrying behind him, came the pup! The creature of many good breeds was accompanying Mr Oliver on his walk. It had been well brushed and was wearing a bright red collar. Like Mr Oliver it took no notice of us, but scampered along beside its new master.

Mr Oliver and the pup were soon inseparable companions, and my friends and I were quite pleased with ourselves. Mr Oliver gave absolutely no indication that he knew where the pup had come from, but when the end-of-term exams were over, and Bimal and I were sure we had failed our Maths paper, we were surprised to find that we had passed after all—with grace marks!

'Good old Olly!' said Bimal. 'So he knew all the time.'

Tata, of course, did not need grace marks; he was a whiz at Maths. But Bimal and I decided we would thank Mr Oliver for his kindness.

'Nothing to thank me for,' said Mr Oliver brusquely. 'I've seen enough of you two in junior school. It's high time you went up to the senior school—and God help you there!'

the goat and the ram

Vikram Seth

An old man and his wife possessed
A zebra of enormous zest,
A white ram of enormous size,
A small black goat with yellow eyes,
Four ducks, a peacock, and a sow,
A gosling, and a purple cow.

The cow gave cream for apple tart,
The zebra drew an apple-cart,
The four fat ducks were good at laying,
The sow excelled at piano-playing,
The gosling could predict the weather,
The peacock flashed a brilliant feather,
But there was really no competing

With ram and goat for over-eating.

They ate all day, they ate all night.
They ate with beastly appetite.
They fed on grapes and grass and grain.
They ate, and paused to eat again.
They ate with pride, as if to balance
Their total lack of other talents.
They raided farmers' kitchens late
At night—and drank the milk—and ate
Both a la carte and table d'hôte.
The ram was nervous; not the goat.
She got the big fat ram to knock
The door down and to break the lock—
And told him: 'Boy, this is the life!'

One night the man said to his wife:
'My dear, that goat and ram mean trouble.
They eat their share—and more than double.
You'd hardly think a small black goat
Could force six bushels down her throat.
She and her friend have eaten all
The apples on our farm this fall.

We can't afford to house and feed
Creatures of such enormous greed.
It's reached the limit. Let's get rid
Of both of them.' And so they did.

Next day the man said: 'Goat and ram—
We've had enough of you. So scram!
Put your belongings in a sack.
And go at once. And don't come back.'
Some of the animals were glad
To see them go, but most were sad,
And the sow snivelled as she played
Dido's lament, 'When I am laid…'

The ram said to the goat: 'Alas—
Now that we've been put out to grass,
Now that we've lost our house and home—
What shall we do, where shall we roam?'
He sobbed and trembled till the goat,
Said rather shortly—and I quote:
'You great big booby, quit this fuss.
Who, after all, is bothering us?
Things aren't that bad. We've not been beaten.

We could have been, but were not, eaten.
Some time we'll find some home somewhere.
Let's keep on walking. What's that there?'

The ram, who was already shivering
At the word 'eaten', started quivering:
For what the goat had pointed out
Was a huge wolf's head—fangs and snout
And bloody mouth with tongue revealed—
Lying discarded in a field.
'I think—' the poor ram started bleating;
'I think we shouldn't talk of eating.
I'm feeling rather, well, upset—'
'Nonsense!' the goat said; 'Go and get
That wolf's head here.' 'Oh,' said the ram,
'I actually believe I am
Going to be sick.' 'Shut up and go!'
The goat commanded him, and so—
Despite the grey ears caked with mud,
The grizzled mane smeared thick with blood,
The yellow teeth of ghastly size,
And the dull, terrifying eyes—
The ram obeyed and, coming back,

Dropped the great wolf's head in the sack.

'Good,' said the goat. 'Who knows, one day
It might prove useful in some way.
Let's go.' And so they kept on walking.
The ram was in no mood for talking.
His heart kept palpitating back
To what he carried in his sack.
But now the day was almost gone,
And the black night was coming on.
And so—disheartened and dismayed—
He whimpered softly: 'I'm afraid.'

'Afraid of what?' 'Of wolves and things—
And beastly bats with wicked wings—
And being all alone at night
With neither food nor firelight
Nor all the farmyard beasts around,'
He said, and made a funny sound—
A sort of gurgle in his throat.
'You great big booby!' said the goat,
'Be quiet. Your depression's draining.
Now dry your face and quit complaining.

Why, isn't that a light out there?'
She pointed with her hoof to where
A distant campfire's golden gleam
Was half-reflected in a stream.
'That clearly is the place to go
If you're afraid of wolves, you know...
We'll be just fine.' And so they turned
To where the distant fire burned.

The timid ram controlled his fear
As they drew near and still more near—
And when at last they reached the cheering
Flame that lit the forest clearing,
Drenched with relief they looked around:
A great round tent stood on the ground,
And by the fire so high and hot,
Preparing porridge in a pot,
Complaining of their hunger-pangs,
Sat three huge wolves with yellow fangs.

'Hello,' the wolves said, 'Glad to meet you.
And gladder still, of course, to eat you.'
Towards the pair the trio padded

And with a grisly grimace added:
'You must forgive our etiquette.
Our porridge isn't ready yet.
It's still a bit too hot to serve.
We'll eat you first, as an hors d'oeuvre.'

At first the goat thought they should flee—
But then she turned, and casually
Said to her friend: 'Hey, Brother Ram,
Are you still hungry? I sure am.
Get that wolf's head out from your sack.
I'd like to have a sundown snack.'
The ram's jaw dropped, but in the end,
Under the sharp gaze of his friend,
He grasped the wolf's head tremblingly
And pulled it out for all to see.

The three great wolves were frightened witless.
Their eyes were glazed, their mouths were spitless.
They breathed a jerky, shallow breath
And shivered with the fear of death.
They stared from goat to ram, and then
Stared back from ram to goat again.

'No, no!' the goat said to the ram,
'That was the wolf who ate the lamb.
Take out the bigger one who tried
To kill the sheep—before he died.'
So the ram put the wolf's head back
And pulled it once more from the sack,
And held it up for all to see.
'This one?' he mumbled fearfully.

The wolves turned green and almost died.
'I've changed my mind,' the goat replied.
'Take out the biggest one of all,
Who killed three oxen in their stall—
The one we slaughtered yesterday
And ate as wolf liver paté.
And, Brother Ram, don't tremble so.
It shows poor taste, as you should know,
To quiver with anticipation
Or to display overt elation
Merely because you've seen your meal.
Think how our friends the wolves must feel.
If they are frightened, they'll grow thinner
Before we've all sat down to dinner.'

So the ram put the wolf's head back
And pulled it once more from the sack.
At this the wolves, whose teeth were chattering,
Whose hearts were numb, whose nerves were shattering,
Looked at the head as if transfixed.
The first wolf said: 'I think I've mixed
Too little water with the oats.
Thick porridge isn't good for goats.
Dear guests, please stay here, and I'll go
Fetch water from the stream below.'
He gave a sort of strangled cough,
Tucked in his tail, and sidled off

The second wolf sat for a minute,
Then murmured: 'Salt's what's lacking in it.
And what is porridge without salt?
It's like—well—whisky without malt—
Heh heh!—or piglets without trotters.
I'll get some from the friendly otters
Whose home is in the stream below.
Wait here—dear guests—I have to go—'
He gave a sort of strangled giggle
And squirmed off swiftly as a squiggle.

The third wolf said: 'Where are those two?
My dear dear friends, what shall I do?
I cannot have you waiting here
While chefs and waiters disappear.
I'll get them back at once. Please stay.
I'll go myself I know the way.'
He gave a sort of strangled howl
And slunk off with a shifty scowl.

'Well,' said the goat, 'we've seen the last
Of our three hosts. Let's break our fast
With what's been cooking in the pot.
I'll bet my tail it's not too hot
Or saltless—or too thick for goats.'
And so they ladled down their throats
Delicious porridge spoon by spoon.
The ram swelled up like a balloon
And lay down on the ground, content.
The goat pulled him inside the tent—
And that was where they spent the night.
Indeed, as of the time I write,
They live there still, secure from harm,
Out of the reach of wolf or farm.

They eat wild strawberries and grass
And drink stream water, clear as glass.
They never argue, never fight.
They never have bad dreams at night.
With moderation and accord
They pass their days, serenely bored.

the stamp album

Sundara Ramaswamy

Rajappa sensed a sudden drop in his popularity. For the past three days everyone had been crowding around Nagarajan.

Rajappa tried to tell them that Nagarajan had become swollen-headed, but no one paid any attention to him. For Nagarajan was generous in sharing the stamp album his uncle had sent from Singapore. The boys gathered around Nagarajan and devoured the album with their eyes till the school bell rang for the morning class; they hovered round him at lunch-break and in the evening invaded his house. Nagarajan showed the album to all of them without a trace of impatience. He only made one stipulation: 'No one must touch the album.' He opened it out on his lap and turned over the pages himself and let everyone gaze to their fill.

The girls wanted to have a look at the album too. The boldest of them, Parvathi, came up to Nagarajan and asked him on behalf of the girls. Nagarajan gave her the album after putting a jacket on it. The album was returned to him in the evening after all the girls had seen it.

No one now mentioned Rajappa's album or paid him any attention.

Once Rajappa's album had been very famous. Rajappa collected stamps in the painstaking way bees collect honey. It was his whole life. He would set out early in the morning to visit other stamp-collectors. He would barter two Pakistans for a solitary U.S.S.R. In the evening he would dump his school books in a corner, stuff a snack in the pocket of his shorts, gulp down a cup of coffee and dash out again. Four miles away a boy had a Canada... He had had the biggest album in his class. The Revenue Officer's son wanted to buy it for twenty-five rupees. The cheek of it! Rajappa retaliated, 'Will you sell your baby brother to me for thirty rupees!' The boys applauded his retort.

But now no one looked at his album. And worse still, they made unfavourable comparisons with Nagarajan's saying his album wasn't fit to hold a candle to Nagarajan's.

Rajappa refused to look at Nagarajan's album. When other boys hovered over it, he turned his face away. But he did try to glance at it through the corner of his eye. It was indeed a beauty! Maybe it didn't have the same stamps as Rajappa's and might even have had not as many as his, but it was the only one of its kind. No local shop had one like it.

Nagarajan's uncle had written his nephew's name in bold letters on the first page of the album: A.S. NAGARAJAN. This was followed by an inscription:

> To the shameless wretch trying to steal this album—See thou my name above? This is my album. It is my property and mine alone as long as the grass is green, the lotus red, the sun rises in the east and sets in the west.

The boys copied the lines in their albums. So did the girls in their books and notebooks.

Rajappa growled, 'Why are you such copycats?'

The boys glared at him and Krishnan retorted, 'Get lost, you jealous worm!'

'Jealous! Me! Why should I be? My album is much

bigger, isn't it?'

'Yours doesn't have stamps like his! Look at the Indonesian beauty—hold it up and see it against the light.'

'He doesn't have the stamps I have!'

'Ha! Show us one he hasn't!'

'You show me one I haven't. Let's have a ten rupee bet.'

'Your album is only fit for the dustbin,' taunted Krishnan. And the boys chanted, 'Garbage album! Garbage album!'

Rajappa realized the futility of continuing the argument.

How long it had taken him to build up his stamp-collection! He had built it stamp by stamp and then the postman had brought this album from Singapore and overnight Nagarajan had become all-important! The boys didn't know the difference between the two albums. And no amount of explaining would make the slightest difference.

Rajappa raged within. He began to hate going to school. How was he to face the boys? Usually on Saturdays and Sundays he hectically stamp hunted but this weekend he barely stirred out of the house. Usually, not a day passed without his turning the pages of his album, over and over again. Even at night he would sneak out of bed to look at the album. But two days had passed and he had not touched it. The sight of it filled him with anger. Compared to Nagarajan's, his album now seemed a bundle of rags.

In the evening Rajappa went to Nagarajan's house. He had made up his mind—he couldn't put up with his ignominy any longer. After all, Nagarajan had only just chanced upon a stamp album. What did he know of the mysteries of stamp-collecting? Or how the experts evaluated them? He probably believed that the bigger the stamp, the more valuable it was. Or one from a powerful country more important than one from a weaker country. After all Nagarajan was only an amateur. Rajappa could easily palm off on him the less valuable stamps and walk away with the good ones. He had fooled many others before. The world of stamp-collecting was rife with cunning and trickery and Nagarajan was only a beginner. Rajappa went straight upstairs to Nagarajan's room. No one stopped him for he was a frequent visitor to the house. Rajappa sat down at Nagarajan's desk. A little later Nagarajan's younger sister, Kamakshi, came in. 'Brother has gone to town,' she said. 'Have you seen his new album?'

Rajappa mumbled something unintelligible. 'It's a real beauty, isn't it? I believe no one else in school has one like it.'

'Who said that?'

'My brother.'

'It's just a big album, no more. Is it enough merely to be oversized?'

Kamakshi didn't reply and walked off.

Rajappa scanned the books littered on the table. His hand grazed against the lock of the table drawer. Almost involuntarily he tugged at it. It was firmly locked. Why not open it? The key lay among the books. Rajappa went over to the staircase and glanced around. No one was in sight. He opened the drawer. Nagarajan's stamp album was right on top. Rajappa turned over the first page and read the inscription. His heart began to pound. He closed the drawer and locked it. He thrust the album into his shorts and let his shirt fall over it. He hurried down the steps and ran home.

On reaching home he hid the album behind his bookshelf. His body felt as though it was on fire, his throat was dry and blood pounded in his head.

Finally at eight in the evening Appu, who lived

opposite, came and told Rajappa that Nagarajan's stamp album was missing Nagarajan and he had gone down to town in the evening and when they returned, the album was gone!

Rajappa didn't utter a word. He prayed that Appu would go away. And when Appu did go away, he hurried to his room and bolted the door. He took out the album from behind the shelf. His hand froze. What if somebody was watching from the shoved the album back behind the shelf.

Rajappa hardly touched his dinner. The family was concerned and asked if he was feeling unwell.

Maybe sleep would bring peace? Rajappa lay down on his bad. But sleep eluded him. What if somebody stumbled upon the hidden album while he was asleep? He got up, took out the album and put it under his pillow.

Rajappa hadn't woken up when Appu appeared in the morning. Appu had just been to Nagarajan's again.

'I'm told you were at his house yesterday.'

Rajappa felt his heart sink. He gave a non-committal nod.

'Kamakshi says you were the only one to call at the house while Nagarajan and I had gone down to town.'

Rajappa detected the suspicion in Appu's tone.

'Nagarajan has been crying all night. His father might send for the police.'

Rajappa didn't say a word.

Nagarajan's father worked in the police superintendent's office. He had only to lift his little finger and the whole police force would be out to trace the album.

Fortunately for Rajappa, Appu's brother arrived to fetch his brother. For a long time after he had left Rajappa sat still on his bed. His father finished breakfast and left for office on his bicycle.

There was a knock at the front door. Was it the police?

Rajappa grabbed the album from under his pillow and ran upstairs and shoved it behind a bookshelf. What if the police made a search? He took it out of the bookshelf, tucked it under his shirt and came downstairs.

Someone was still knocking on the door. Rajappa's mother shouted from the kitchen, 'Why don't you open the door?' She was sure to go and unbolt it herself in a few seconds.

Rajappa ran to the back of the house. He went into the bathroom and closed the door. There was a large oven in the bathroom for heating the bath-water. Rajappa threw the album in the fire. The album burned; and with it all the precious stamps that were unavailable anywhere. Tears filled Rajappa's eyes.

Mother was shouting, 'Hurry up! Nagarajan has come to see you.'

Rajappa took off his shorts and wrapping himself with a wet towel came out of the bathroom. He put on a fresh shirt and shorts and went upstairs. Nagarajan was sitting in a chair.

'My stamp album is lost,' Nagarajan said in a broken voice. His face was grief-stricken and his eyes red-rimmed and swollen with hours of crying.

'Where had you kept it?' Rajappa asked.

'I am sure I had put it in the table drawer. I had locked the drawer too. I went out for a short while and when I returned it was gone.'

Tears streamed down his face. Rajappa felt so guilty he could hardly look at his friend. 'Don't cry,' he mumbled.

But the more he tried to console Nagarajan the more the boy cried.

Rajappa ran downstairs and was back in a moment. He had his stamp album in his arms.

'Nagarajan, here's my album. It's yours. Don't look at

me in that way! I mean it, really. The album is for you.'

'You're joking…'

'No. I am giving it to you. Honestly. It's all yours from today. Keep it.'

Nagarajan couldn't believe his eyes. Rajappa giving his album away! But Rajappa kept urging him to take it. 'What about you?' Nagarajan asked.

'I don't want it any more.'

'Not even a stamp?'

'No, not even one.'

'But how will you live without your stamps?'

Rajappa's eyes brimmed with tears.

'Don't cry, Rajappa. You don't have to give away your stamp album. Keep it. You worked so hard on it.'

'No, you keep it. It's for you. Take it home. Please take it and go away,' screamed Rajappa.

Nagarajan was baffled. He took the album and came down. Rajappa followed him, wiping his tears with his shirt-end.

They stood at the door. 'Thank you,' Nagarajan said. 'Bye.'

Nagarajan had stepped into the street when Rajappa called out to him.

Nagarajan turned.

'Please…please give me the album just for tonight. I will hand it back to you tomorrow morning.'

Nagarajan agreed and went away.

Rajappa climbed the stairs and bolted the door of his room. Holding the album tightly, he sobbed his heart out.

Translated from the Tamil by Ashokamitran

the thak man-eater

Jim Corbett

A man-eating tigress is on the prowl near the village of Thak in Kumaon (in present day Uttarakhand). Several people have already been killed. Jim Corbett has been summoned by the forest department to deal with this menace but it is not an easy task to bring the man-eater down.

—Editor

When all my visitors, including the Headman, had gone, and I was having breakfast, my servant informed me that the Headman of Sem had come to the camp the previous evening and had left word for me that his wife, while cutting grass near the hut where his mother had been killed, had come on a blood trail, and that he would wait for me near the ford over the

Ladhya in the morning. So after breakfast I set out to investigate this trail.

While I was fording the river I saw four men hurrying towards me, and as soon as I was on dry land they told me that when they were coming down the hill above Sem they had heard a tiger calling across the valley on the hill between Chuka and Thak. The noise of the water had prevented my hearing the call. I told the men that I was on my way to Sem and would return to Chuka shortly, and left them.

The Headman was waiting for me near his house, and his wife took me to where she had seen the blood trail the previous day. The trail, after continuing along a field for a short distance, crossed some big rocks, on one of which I found the hairs of a kakar. A little further on I found the pug marks of a big male leopard, and while I was looking at them I heard a tiger call. Telling my companions to sit down and remain quiet, I listened, in order to locate the tiger. Presently I heard the call again, and thereafter it was repeated at intervals of about two minutes.

It was the tigress calling and I located her as being five hundred yards below Thak and in the deep ravine which, starting from the spring under the mango tree, runs parallel to the path and crosses it at its junction with the Kumaya Chak path.

Telling the Headman that the leopard would have to wait to be shot at a more convenient time, I set off as hard as I could go for camp, picking up at the ford the four men who were waiting for my company to Chuka.

On reaching camp I found a crowd of men round my tent, most of them sawyers from Delhi, but including the petty contractors, agents, clerks, timekeepers, and gangmen of the financier who had taken up the timber and road construction contracts in the Ladhya valley. These men had come to see me in connexion with my stay at Chuka. They informed me that many of the hillmen carrying timber and working on the road had left for their homes that morning and that if I left Chuka on 1st December, as they had heard I intended doing, the entire labour force, including themselves, would leave on the same day; for already they were too frightened to eat or sleep, and no one would dare to remain in the valley after I had gone. It was then the morning of 29th November and I told the men that I still had two days and two nights and that much could happen in that time, but that in any case it would not be possible for me to prolong my stay beyond the morning of the 1st.

The tigress had by now stopped calling, and when my servant had put up something for me to eat I set out for Thak, intending, if the tigress called again and I could locate her position, to try to stalk her; and if she did not call again, to sit up over the buffalo. I found her tracks on the path and saw where she had entered the ravine, and though I stopped repeatedly on my way up to Thak and listened I did not hear her again. So a little before sunset I ate the biscuits and drank the bottle of tea I had brought with me, and then climbed into the almond tree and took my seat on the few strands of rope that had to serve me as a machan. On this occasion the magpies were absent, so I was unable to get the hour or two's sleep the birds had enabled me to get the previous evening.

If a tiger fails to return ·to its kill the first night it does not necessarily mean that the kill has been abandoned. I have on occasions seen a tiger return on the tenth night and eat what could no longer be described as fresh. On the present occasion, however, I was not sitting over a kill, but over an animal that the tigress had found dead and off which she had made a small meal, and had she not been a man-eater I would not have considered the chance of her returning the second night good enough to justify spending a whole night in a tree when she had not taken sufficient interest in the dead buffalo to return to it the first night. It was therefore with very little hope of getting a shot that I sat on the tree from sunset to sunrise, and though the time I spent was not as long as it had been the previous night, my discomfort was very much greater, for the ropes I was sitting on cut into me, and a cold wind that started blowing shortly after moonrise and continued throughout the night chilled me to the bone. On this second night I heard no jungle or other sounds nor did the sambur and her young one come out to feed on the fields. As daylight was succeeding moonlight I thought I heard a tiger call in the distance, but could not be sure of the sound or of its direction.

When I got back to camp my servant had a cup of tea and a hot bath ready for me, but before I could indulge in the latter—my 40-lb. tent was not big enough for me to bathe in—I had to get rid of the excited throng of people who were clamouring to tell me their experiences of the night before: It appeared that shortly after moonrise the tigress had started calling close to Chuka, and after calling at intervals for a couple of hours had gone off in the direction of the labour camps at Kumaya Chak. The men in these camps, hearing her coming, started shouting to try to drive her away, but so far from having this effect the shouting only infuriated her the more and she demonstrated in front of the camps until she had cowed the men into silence. Having accomplished this she spent the rest of the night between the labour camps and Chuka, daring all and sundry to shout at her. Towards morning she had gone away in the direction of Thak, and my informants were surprised and very disappointed that I had not met her.

This was my last day of man-eater hunting, and though I was badly in need of rest and sleep, I decided to spend what was left of it in one last attempt to get in touch with the tigress.

The people not only of Chuka and Sem but of all the surrounding villages, and especially the men from Talla Des where some years previously I had shot three man-eaters, were very anxious that I should try sitting up over a live goat, for, said they, 'All hill tigers eat goats, and as you have had no luck with buffaloes, why not try a goat?' More to humour them than with any hope of getting a shot, I consented to spend this last day in sitting up over the two goats I had already purchased for this purpose.

I was convinced that no matter where the tigress wandered to at night her headquarters were at Thak, so at midday, taking the two goats, and accompanied by four of my men, I set out for Thak.

The path from Chuka to Thak, as I have already mentioned, runs up a very steep ridge. A quarter of a mile on this side of Thak the path leaves the ridge, and crosses a more or less flat bit of ground which extends right up to the mango tree. For its whole length across this flat ground the path passes through dense brushwood, and is crossed by two narrow ravines which run east and join the main ravine. Midway between these two ravines, and a hundred yards from the tree I had sat in the previous two nights, there is a giant almond tree; this tree had been my objective when I left camp. The path passes right under the tree and I thought that if I climbed half-way up not only should I be able to see the two goats, one of which I intended tying at the edge of the main ravine and the other at the foot of the hill to the right, but I should also be able to see the dead buffalo. As all three of these points were at some distance from the tree, I armed myself with an accurate .275 rifle, in addition to the 450/400 rifle which I took for an emergency.

I found the climb up from Chuka on this last day very trying, and I had just reached the spot where the path leaves the ridge for the flat ground, when the tigress called about a hundred and fifty yards to my left. The ground here was covered with dense undergrowth and trees interlaced with creepers, and was cut up by narrow and deep ravines, and strewn over with enormous boulders—a very unsuitable place in which to stalk a man-eater. However, before deciding on what action I should take it was necessary to know whether the tigress was lying down, as she very well might be, for it was then 1 p.m., or whether she was on the move and if so in what direction. So making the men sit down behind me I listened, and presently the call was repeated; she had moved some fifty yards, and appeared to be going up the main ravine in the direction of Thak.

This was very encouraging, for the tree I had selected to sit in was only fifty yards from the ravine. After enjoining silence on the men and telling them to keep close behind me, we hurried along the path. We had about two hundred yards to go to reach the tree and had covered half the distance when, as we approached a spot where the path was bordered on both sides by dense brushwood, a covey of kaleege pheasants rose out of the brushwood and went screaming away. I knelt down and covered the path for a few minutes, but as nothing happened we went cautiously forward and reached the tree without further incident. As quickly and as silently as possible one goat was tied at the edge of the ravine, while the other was tied at the foot of the hill to the right; then I took the men to the edge of the cultivated land and told them to stay in the upper veranda of the Headman's house until I fetched them, and ran back to the tree. I climbed to a height of forty feet, and pulled the rifle up after me with a cord I had brought for the purpose. Not only were the two goats visible from my seat, one at a range of seventy and the other at a range of sixty yards, but I could also see part of the buffalo, and as the .275 rifle was very accurate I felt sure I could kill the tigress if she showed up anywhere on the ground I was overlooking.

The two goats had lived together ever since I had

purchased them on my previous visit, and, being separated now, were calling lustily to each other. Under normal conditions a goat can be heard at a distance of four hundred yards, but here the conditions were not normal, for the goats were tied on the side of a hill down which a strong wind was blowing, and even if the tigress had moved after I had heard her, it was impossible for her not to hear them. If she was hungry, as I had every reason to believe she was, there was a very good chance of my getting a shot.

After I had been on the tree for ten minutes a kakar barked near the spot the pheasants had risen from. For a minute or two my hopes rose sky-high and then dropped back to earth, for the kakar barked only three times and ended on a note of inquiry; evidently there was a snake in the scrub which neither he nor the pheasants liked the look of.

My seat was not uncomfortable and the sun was pleasingly warm, so for the next three hours I remained in the tree without any discomfort. At 4 p.m. the sun went down behind the high hill above Thak and thereafter the wind became unbearably cold. For an hour I stood the discomfort, and then decided to give up, for the cold had brought on an attack of ague, and if the tigress came now it would not be possible for me to hit her. I retied the cord to the rifle and let it down, climbed down myself and walked to the edge of the cultivated land to call up my men.

~

There are few people, I imagine, who have not experienced that feeling of depression that follows failure to accomplish any thing they have set out to do. The road back to camp after a strenuous day when the *chukor* (hill partridge) bag is full is only a step compared with the same road which one plods over, mile after weary mile, when the bag is empty, and if this feeling of depression has ever assailed you at the end of a single day, and when the quarry has only been *chukor*, you will have some idea of the depth of my depression that evening when, after calling up my men and untying the goats, I set off on my two-mile walk to camp, for my effort had not been of a single day or my quarry a few birds, nor did my failure concern only myself.

Excluding the time spent on the journeys from and to home, I had been on the heels of the man-eater from

23rd October to 7th November, and again from 24th to 30th November, and it is only those of you who have walked in fear of having the teeth of a tiger meet in your throat who will have any idea of the effect on one's nerves of days and weeks of such anticipation.

Then again my quarry was a man-eater, and my failure to shoot it would very gravely affect everyone who was working in, or whose homes were in, that area. Already work in the forests had been stopped, and the entire population of the largest village in the district had abandoned their homes. Bad as the conditions were they would undoubtedly get worse if the maneater was not killed, for the entire labour force could not afford to stop work indefinitely, nor could the population of surrounding villages afford to abandon their homes and their cultivation as the more prosperous people of Thak had been able to do.

The tigress had long since lost her natural fear of human beings as was abundantly evident from her having carried away a girl picking up mangoes in a field close to where several men were working, killing a woman near the door of her house, dragging a man off a tree in the heart of a village, and, the previous night, cowing a few thousand men into silence. And here was I, who knew full well what the presence of a man-eater meant to the permanent and to the temporary inhabitants and to all the people who passed through the district on their way to the markets at the foot-hills or the temples at Punagiri, plodding down to camp on what I had promised others would be my last day of man-eater hunting; reason enough for a depression of soul which I felt would remain with me for the rest of my days. Gladly at that moment would I have bartered the success that had attended thirty-two years of man-eater hunting for one unhurried shot at the tigress.

I have told you of some of the attempts I made during this period of seven days and seven nights to get a shot at the tigress, but these were by no means the only attempts I made. I knew that I was being watched and followed, and every time I went through the two miles of jungle between my camp and Thak I tried every trick I have learnt in a lifetime spent in the jungles to outwit the tigress. Bitter though my disappointment was, I felt that my failure was not in any way due to anything I had done or left undone.

My men when they rejoined me said that, an hour after the kakar had barked, they had heard the tigress calling a long way off but were not sure of the direction. Quite evidently the tigress had as little interest in goats as she had in buffaloes, but even so it was unusual for her to have moved at that time of day from a locality in which she was thoroughly at home, unless she had been attracted away by some sound which neither I nor my men had heard; however that may have been, it was quite evident that she had gone, and as there was nothing further that I could do I set off on my weary tramp to camp.

The path, as I have already mentioned, joins the ridge that runs down to Chuka a quarter of a mile from Thak, and when I now got to this spot where the ridge is only a few feet wide and from where a view is obtained of the two great ravines that run down to the Ladhya river, I heard the tigress call once and again across the valley on my left. She was a little above and to the left of Kumaya Chak, and a few hundred yards below the Kot Kindri ridge on which the men working in that area had built themselves grass shelters.

Here was an opportunity, admittedly forlorn and unquestionably desperate, of getting a shot; still it was an opportunity and the last I should ever have, and the question was, whether or not I was justified in taking it.

When I got down from the tree I had one hour in which to get back to camp before dark. Calling up the men, hearing what they had to say, collecting the goats and walking to the ridge had taken about thirty minutes, and judging from the position of the sun which was now casting a red glow on the peaks of the Nepal hills, I calculated I had roughly half an hour's daylight in hand. This time factor, or perhaps it would be more correct to say light factor, was all-important, for if I took the opportunity that offered, on it would depend the lives of five men.

The tigress was a mile away and the intervening ground was densely wooded, strewn over with great rocks and cut up by a number of deep nullahs, but she could cover the distance well within the half-hour—if she wanted to. The question I had to decide was, whether or not I should try to call her up. If I called and she heard me, and came while it was still daylight and gave me a shot, all would be well; on the other hand, if she came and did not give me a shot some of us would not reach camp, for we had nearly two miles to go and the path the whole way ran through heavy jungle, and was bordered in some places by big rocks, and in others by dense brushwood. It was useless to consult the men, for none of them had ever been in a jungle before coming on this trip, so the decision would have to be mine.

I decided to try to call up the tigress.

Handing my rifle over to one of the men I waited until the tigress called again and, cupping my hands round my mouth and filling my lungs to their utmost limit, sent an answering call over the valley. Back came her call and thereafter, for several minutes, call answered call. She would come, had in fact already started, and if she arrived while there was light to shoot by, all the advantages would be on my side, for I had the selecting of the ground on which it would best suit me to meet her. November is the mating season for tigers and it was evident that for the past forty-eight hours she had been rampaging through the jungles in search of a mate, and that now, on hearing what she thought was a tiger answering her mating call, she would lose no time in joining him.

Four hundred yards down the ridge the path runs for

fifty yards across a flat bit of ground. At the far right-hand side of this flat ground the path skirts a big rock and then drops steeply, and continues in a series of hairpin bends, down to the next bend. It was at this rock I decided to meet the tigress, and on my way down to it I called several times to let her know I was changing my position, and also to keep in touch with her.

I want you now to have a clear picture of the ground in your mind, to enable you to follow the subsequent events. Imagine then a rectangular piece of ground forty yards wide and eighty yards long, ending in a more or less perpendicular rock face. The path coming down from Thak runs on to this ground at its short or south end, and after continuing down the centre for twenty-five yards bends to the right and leaves the rectangle on its long or east side. At the point where the path leaves the flat ground there is a rock about four feet high. From a little beyond where the path bends to the right, a ridge of rock, three or four feet high, rises and extends to the north side of the rectangle, where the ground falls away in a perpendicular rock face. On the near or path side of this low ridge there is a dense line of bushes approaching to within ten feet of the four-foot high rock

I have mentioned. The rest of the rectangle is grown over with trees, scattered bushes, and short grass.

It was my intention to lie on the path by the side of the rock and shoot the tigress as she approached me, but when I tried this position I found it would not be possible for me to see her until she was within two or three yards, and further, that she could get at me either round the rock or through the scattered bushes on my left without my seeing her at all. Projecting out of the rock, from the side opposite to that from which I expected the tigress to approach, there was a narrow ledge. By sitting sideways I found I could get a little of my bottom on the ledge, and by putting my left hand flat on the top of the rounded rock and stretching out my right leg to its full extent and touching the ground with my toes, retain my position on it. The men and goats I placed immediately behind, and ten to twelve feet below me.

The stage was now set for the reception of the tigress, who while these preparations were being made had approached to within three hundred yards. Sending out one final call to give her direction, I looked round to see if my men were all right.

The spectacle these men presented would under other

circumstances have been ludicrous, but was here tragic. Sitting in a tight little circle with their knees drawn up and their heads together, with the goats burrowing in under them, they had that look of intense expectancy on their screwed-up features that one sees on the faces of spectators waiting to hear a big gun go off. From the time we had first heard the tigress from the ridge, neither the men nor the goats had made a sound, beyond one suppressed cough. They were probably by now frozen with fear—as well they might be—and even if they were I take my hat off to those four men who had the courage to do what I, had I been in their shoes, would not have dreamt of doing. For seven days they had been hearing the most exaggerated and blood-curdling tales of this fearsome beast that had kept them awake the past two nights, and now, while darkness was coming on, and sitting unarmed in a position where they could see nothing, they were listening to the man-eater drawing nearer and nearer; greater courage, and greater faith, it is not possible to conceive.

The fact that I could not hold my rifle, a D.B. 450/400, with my left hand (which I was using to retain my precarious seat on the ledge) was causing me some uneasiness, for apart from the fear of the rifle slipping on the rounded top of the rock—I had folded my handkerchief and placed the rifle on it to try to prevent this—I did not know what would be the effect of the recoil of a high velocity rifle fired in this position. The rifle was pointing along the path, in which there was a hump, and it was my intention to fire into the tigress's face immediately it appeared over this hump, which was twenty feet from the rock.

The tigress, however, did not keep to the contour of the hill, which would have brought her out on the path a little beyond the hump, but crossed a deep ravine and came straight towards where she had heard my last call, at an angle which I can best describe as one o'clock. This manoeuvre put the low ridge of rock, over which I could not see, between us. She had located the direction of my last call with great accuracy, but had misjudged the distance, and not finding her prospective mate at the spot she had expected him to be, she was now working herself up into a perfect fury, and you will have some idea of what the fury of a tigress in her condition can be when I tell you that not many miles from my home a tigress on one occasion closed a public road for a whole week, attacking everything that attempted to go along it, including a string of camels, until she was finally joined by a mate.

I know of no sound more liable to fret one's nerves than the calling of an unseen tiger at close range. What effect this appalling sound was having on my men I was frightened to think, and if they had gone screaming down the hill I should not have been at all surprised, for even though I had the heel of a good rifle to my shoulder and the stock against my cheek I felt like screaming myself.

But even more frightening than this continuous calling was the fading out of the light. Another few seconds, ten or fifteen at the most, and it would be too dark to see my sights, and we should then be at the mercy of a man-eater, plus a tigress wanting a mate. Something would have to be done, and done in a hurry if we were not to be massacred, and the only thing I could think of was to call.

The tigress was now so close that I could hear the intake of her breath each time before she called, and as she again filled her lungs, I did the same with mine, and we called simultaneously. The effect was startlingly instantaneous. Without a second's hesitation she came tramping with quick steps through the dead leaves, over the low ridge and into the bushes a little to my right front, and just as I was expecting her to walk right on top of me she stopped, and the next moment the full blast of her deep-throated call struck me in the face and would have carried the hat off my head had I been wearing one. A second's pause, then again quick steps; a glimpse of her as she passed between two bushes, and then she stepped right out into the open, and, looking into my face, stopped dead.

By great and unexpected good luck the half-dozen steps the tigress took to her right front carried her almost to the exact spot at which my rifle was pointing. Had she continued in the direction in which she was coming before her last call, my story—if written—would have had a different ending, for it would have been as impossible to slew the rifle on the rounded top of the rock as it would have been to lift and fire it with one hand.

Owing to the nearness of the tigress, and the fading light, all that I could see of her was her head. My first bullet caught her under the right eye and the second, fired more by accident than with intent, took her in the throat and she came to rest with her nose against the rock. The recoil from the right barrel loosened my hold on the rock and knocked me off the ledge, and the recoil from the left barrel, fired while I was in the air, brought the rifle up in violent contact with my jaw and sent me heels over head right on top of the men and goats. Once again I take my hat off to those four men for, not knowing but what the tigress was going to land on them next, they caught me as I fell and saved me from injury and my rifle from being broken.

When I had freed myself from the tangle of human and goat legs I took the .275 rifle from the man who was holding it, rammed a clip of cartridges into the magazine and sent a stream of five bullets singing over the valley and across the Sarda into Nepal. Two shots, to the thousands of men in the valley and in the surrounding villages who were anxiously listening for the sound of my rifle, might mean anything, but two shots followed by five more, spaced at regular intervals of five seconds, could only be interpreted as conveying one message, and that was, that the man-eater was dead.

I had not spoken to my men from the time we had first heard the tigress from the ridge. On my telling them now that she was dead and that there was no longer any reason for us to be afraid, they did not appear to be able to take in what I was saying, so I told them to go up and have a look while I found and lit a cigarette. Very cautiously they climbed up to the rock, but went no further for, as I have told you, the tigress was touching the other side of it. Late in camp that night, while sitting round a camp-fire, and relating their experiences to relays of eager listeners, their narrative invariably ended up with, 'and then the tiger whose roaring had turned our livers into water hit the sahib on the head and knocked him down on top of us and if you don't believe us, go and look at his face.' A mirror is superfluous in camp and even if I had one it could not have made the swelling on my jaw, which put me on milk diet for several days, look as large and as painful as it felt.

By the time a sapling had been felled and the tigress lashed to it, lights were beginning to show in the Ladhya valley and in all the surrounding camps and villages. The four men were very anxious to have the honour of carrying the tigress to camp, but the task was beyond them; so I left them and set off for help.

In my three visits to Chuka during the past eight months I had been along this path many times by day and always with a loaded rifle in my hands, and now I was stumbling down in the dark, unarmed, my only anxiety being to avoid a fall. If the greatest happiness one can experience is the sudden cessation of great pain, then the second greatest happiness is undoubtedly the sudden cessation of great fear. One short hour previously it would have taken wild elephants to have dragged from their homes and camps the men who now, singing and shouting, were converging from every direction, singly and in groups, on the path leading to Thak. Some of the men of this rapidly growing crowd went up the path to help carry in the tigress, while others accompanied me on my way to camp, and would have carried me had I permitted them. Progress was slow, for frequent halts had to be made to allow each group of new arrivals to express their gratitude in their own particular way. This gave the party carrying the tigress time to catch us up, and we entered the village together. I will not attempt to describe the welcome my men and I received, or the scenes I witnessed at Chuka that night, for having lived the greater part of my life in the jungles I have not the ability to paint word-pictures.

A hayrick was dismantled and the tigress laid on it,

and an enormous bonfire made from driftwood close at hand to light up the scene and for warmth, for the night was dark and cold with a north wind blowing. Round about midnight my servant, assisted by the Headman of Thak and Kunwar Singh, near whose house I was camped, persuaded the crowd to return to their respective villages and labour camps, telling them they would have ample opportunity of feasting their eyes on the tigress the following day. Before leaving himself, the Headman of Thak told me he would send word in the morning to the people of Thak to return to their village. This he did, and two days later the entire population returned to their homes, and have lived in peace ever since.

After my midnight dinner I sent for Kunwar Singh and told him that in order to reach home on the promised date I should have to start in a few hours, and that he would have to explain to the people in the morning why I had gone. This he promised to do, and I then started to skin the tigress. Skinning a tiger with a pocket-knife is a long job, but it gives one an opportunity of examining the animal that one would otherwise not get, and in the case of man-eaters enables one to ascertain, more or less accurately, the reason for the animal having become a man-eater.

The tigress was a comparatively young animal and in the perfect condition one would expect her to be at the beginning of the mating season. Her dark winter coat was without a blemish, and in spite of her having so persistently refused the meals I had provided for her she was encased in fat. She had two old gunshot wounds, neither of which showed on her skin. The one in her left shoulder, caused by several pellets of homemade buckshot, had become septic, and when healing the skin, over quite a large surface, had adhered permanently to the flesh. To what extent this wound had incapacitated her it would have been difficult to say, but it had evidently taken a very long time to heal, and could quite reasonably have been the cause of her having become a man-eater. The second wound, which was in her right shoulder, had also been caused by a charge of buckshot but had healed without becoming septic. These two wounds received over kills in the days before she had become a man eater were quite sufficient reason for her not having returned to the human and other kills I had sat over.

After having skinned the tigress I bathed and dressed, and though my face was swollen and painful and I had twenty miles of rough going before me, I left Chuka walking on air, while the thousands of men in and around the valley were peacefully sleeping.

I have come to the end of the jungle stories I set out tell you and I have also come near the end of my man-eater hunting career.

I have had a long spell and count myself fortunate in having walked out on my own feet and not been carried out on a cradle in the manner and condition of the man of Thak.

There have been occasions when life has hung by a thread and others when a light purse and disease resulting from exposure and strain have made the going difficult, but for all these occasions I am amply rewarded if my hunting has resulted in saving one human life.

the library

Paul Zacharia

One day, a little girl called Aruna brought home a book from the library in her village. She was only twelve, but when she searched for books, she did not look in the Children's Books cupboard alone. She liked books for adults just as much as she liked children's books. Therefore she read Mali's stories and Palliyara Shreedharan's 'Wonders of Math' (*Kanakkuviseshangal*). But she also read with the same happy eagerness the books of Basheer, Madhavikkutty, the stories of Mundoor Krishnan Kutty, the poems of P. Kunhiraman Nair, Vailoppilly, Ayyappa Panikker, and so on.

Once, Aruna leapt headlong into an adventure. She borrowed the Malayalam translation of *War and Peace* from the library. Handing her that volume of thousand-odd pages which weighed a whole kilo, the secretary of the library asked her, 'Hey Aruna, will you be able to read it all? But first of all, how are you going to carry this home?'

Aruna felt a bit bashful. She said, 'I am going to try, Uncle.'

She managed to lug it home and started reading it. It had to be renewed two times in the library register! Father, Mother, Grandma, Aruna's older sister and younger brother—all of them pressed their fingers on their noses, so surprised were they. But Aruna read all of *War and Peace* in five weeks. Then she went straight into the library carrying the fat book on her shoulder, with a broad smile that filled her face and the whole new world that brimmed and bubbled within her. The secretary was very pleased indeed. He said, 'Smart girl! You must surely tell me the story, all right? Because I can't read it all. And I agree—from now, you aren't a little child!' Aruna blushed again.

But she was actually just a little child. Each book took her little mind towards new experiences and knowledge that made it soar higher and higher, filling it with thrills of pleasure. Many books, she read over and over again.

Each time, they conjured up magical rivulets from which pleasurable feelings, old and new, burst out and flowed all around her. She did not know that she was a bookworm. No one called her that. If she knew, Aruna would surely say, oh, the life of a worm, what fun!

The library was a tiny one, in a faraway village and so it did not have many books. But it was chockful with stories and novels and history and philosophy and autobiography and poetry and drama and essays and humor—a little bit of everything, and children's books too. Because Aruna had finished reading most of the books over a long time, she read many books again. As I told you before, the fun of reading a book all over once more is special indeed. By the time we reach page fifteen, we already know about the wonders that await us on page twenty-five! And then the thing to do is to rush headfirst towards them.

But there was a particular day on which Aruna went wild with joy. That day came only once a year; it was the day on which the library received its yearly grant and the secretary went to the town and got new books. On that day, Aruna would somehow reach the library before the bus that brought him back reached the village. She would watch him as he walked by after he had gotten off the bus carrying the bundles of new books. Like an eager sprite, she would hover in a corner, waiting for the moment in which he got up to open the bundles after resting a bit under the fan and having a sip of water. When he started cutting up the jute cord that bound the books with a pen-knife, she would draw closer. She would then lend a hand in the job of getting the books out. Each time she picked up a book, a wave of hope would swathe her. The crisp scent of brand-new books would rise up from the bundles like fragrance from a garden and leave her giddy. The colours and images of their covers would throb in front of her eyes like an enchanted world. The secretary never said anything. He welcomed her help with a smile. She would sweep up the old newspaper-wrappings of the bundles and the cut jute cord into the dust-bin. And would go up to the table where the new books were piled, run her hands on them, and dream. The secretary would then smile and tell her, 'Oh, thanks a lot, Aruna! Now you can go home. I'll enter all these books in our register in two or three days and give them a number. Then you can start!' But Aruna would not go. She would loiter there, leafing through the new books. The secretary would smile again. 'Okay, Aruna, you want a new book, right? You are making me break the rule every year! Take one, but keep mum about it. And bring it back tomorrow.' Without a moment's delay, she would close her eyes and pick her book. And then she would run home, as fast as an arrow.

She will find out what the book is about only when she reaches home! And that is the golden moment in the life of Aruna the Bookworm!

But the book that she found today wasn't one of this kind. It was from the novel section, and she had not seen it before. It lay tumbled behind the highest row on the shelf, which she could reach only with a lot of effort. She saw it lying behind the row when she pulled out three or four books together. She took it out, dusted it. It had no cover and its front pages which carried the author's and publisher's names were missing. Aruna examined the book. How did the pages go missing? Because the cover and the first pages were gone, the thread that held the pages together could be seen. When she glanced at the book trying to guess what story it told, she realized that the first sentence on the first page was incomplete. It began on an earlier, missing page. She checked the page numbers: the first sixteen pages were gone. This book now began from the seventeenth. Then she looked at the last page. The last sentence too was incomplete; its other half was somewhere else. The last page was page number 102. Who knows how many remained? So there! There lay in her hands a book with no beginning and no end! Never mind, she thought, let me read what happened between the unknown beginning and unknown end, and went up to the secretary's desk. He took a look at it and said, 'Aruna, this book has no name and no place, where did you get it from?'

'Uncle, it was lying behind the topmost row in the Novels section. I am seeing it for the first time,' replied Aruna.

He smiled and continued, 'If it hasn't been spotted even by you, then it must be the magical book of this library.' He tried to locate the register number somewhere inside but couldn't find even the library's seal on any page. 'That's funny,' said the secretary, 'What will I write in the register? No name, no number, no beginning, no end. Okay, let's do something ... I'll mark it with the seal, give it a temporary number and write it down in the register.'

When he handed her the book after he had marked and numbered it, the secretary asked Aruna, 'But how will you read this novel with no start and no finish?'

'Let me try, Uncle,' she said.

She returned home, did her homework, studied for school, finished up her chores, ate, bathed, and sat down to read the book on the back veranda, stretching her legs out.

She raced ahead from the broken sentence on the first page. When she covered a few more pages, Aruna began to make sense of the happenings in the book. That is, early in the morning, twelve-year-old Ashok went for his maths tuitions at the home of a teacher named Basheer through a narrow lane. A few cats would be hanging about there. Free, liberated alley-cats! No one raised them. They bore the weight of their lives by themselves. They were waiting for the fish-seller lady. She would throw them the waste after she cleaned fish for housewives. They were waiting for that breakfast.

Aruna liked it. That's great! Alley-cats are free, aren't they? And besides, they deal with life on their own terms. And what about me, Aruna thought. Well, I too do some things on my own terms, she told herself. But it was all of a sudden that shocking turns appeared in the story. That is, Ashok is on his way to tuition one morning when he hears a soft, small voice calling to him: 'Child!'

He looks around, amazed. No one is to be seen. When he starts to walk, again, the voice: 'Child! A moment please!' That took him completely by surprise. It was a black cat, sitting on an empty flower-pot on top of the wall, who was calling to him!

Aruna shifted a bit. She folded her legs which were stretched, relaxed. A deep sigh escaped her. She cast an unseeing look all around. Bit her lip. The book had taken over her now. The story now held her by the wrist and zipped ahead. She became oblivious of the hens feasting away on the coconut pieces left to dry in the sun outside, to what her mother asked her a couple of times, to the big crow-fight on top of the mango tree which climaxed in two opponents falling to the ground, to her pet dog Nanan who stood beside her hopefully for some time, wagging his tail lovingly.

The black cat tells Ashok something utterly astonishing. That it was a time-traveller—that is, someone who travels back and forth through time using the powers of scientific knowledge. It came from a planet which belonged to another sun, some 3,000 light-years away from our own solar system; it was the fifth planet of that solar system. It spotted our Earth while travelling through time and liked it. It walked through the time of our Earth. But in the year 7018 on Earth, it had an accident. In the Earth of that time, cats were the only residents. Therefore it too took on a cat-body. But it got caught in a war between cats and had to flee hastily. It happened to descend on the Earth of these times, and on this street where there was a fish-seller lady. But in the hurry to get away, both the button that allowed it to travel through time-paths and the button that would have let it return to its original form fell on the ground. Before it could retrieve them, it was zooming away on the time-pathway.

But it did see a kitten pick up the two buttons with its mouth and take them to the temple of the God of the Cats. Here, it was observing Ashok since some days. It took a liking to him. It wanted to ask for a favour. It couldn't return to year 7018 as you can enter one time only once. But it could send Ashok there. Could Ashok become a time-traveller and get it those two buttons from that time?

Ashok needn't get into the cat-war. All he had to do was return to the moment in which the kitten stepped into the temple. The rest would depend upon luck, and it would all be between the kitten and Ashok. If the buttons could not be restored to the time-traveller, it would have to live on this road for the rest of its life. Its family and its home, waiting light-years away, would wait in vain. Ashok needs only a few seconds to travel through time and return. Within those few seconds, millions and millions of eras would have passed—which is another matter. Ashok agrees when he gets to know that he requires just a few moments and that he won't be late for his tuitions at the teacher's.

The story heats up then. Aruna turned and pressed the wall with both feet. She and the book became one and the same.

Ashok loses his way and wanders through many eras in the future. How wondrous, the sights that he sees! What changes! Earth swallowed by the fog, the sand-jungle, and then the sea. He found times when there was no life at all on Earth. Times when the ants were sole masters of the planet. Times in which human beings shrunk to just a mass of brains and lived in special tissue-cultures and chemical solutions. And thus as Ashok was sweeping through time as an atom-sized hurricane, he saw a beautiful planet. He descended into it. It looked like the Earth. Human beings, just like us. But not us. Their faces and eyes carried other knowledge. He was walking through the street of a small city. When he turned the street, he saw a lone boy walking this side. His form looked familiar. He had note-books and other books. As they neared each other, Ashok's eyes expanded with sheer surprise. The other boy's eyes mirrored Ashok's amazed look. Ashok was seeing himself. And then Ashok … Aruna sprinted to the next page like a champion racer. But…her fingers could grab only empty air. The next page was *gone* somewhere, sometime, for some reason, wasn't it? Shaken with disappointment, she turned over the book and examined it in and out. What use? The page simply wasn't there. She went back to Page 17, that was all. Aruna gazed at the book, feeling terribly sad. Then a short scream left her and she bent over on the floor covering her face with her hands. And still not able to let go of her sadness, she lay down on the floor of the veranda all curled up, still holding the book. Oh, what a terrible pity! What would have happened next? Oh— imagine, I meeting myself! She slipped into sleep when she was thinking about what would happen, in that case.

Suddenly, a dream entered her sleep. She was reading the novel about the black cat and had reached the last page. And then Ashok—she had passed these words too and gone into the next page. There the page was, in her hands! There were many pages that followed this one, too. They will tell me all about how Ashok retrieved the buttons and returned home, and how the black cat went back to his time, she thought happily. And then she got back to the sentence that began with 'And then Ashok ...' and started to read all of it. Ashok asked the child who came towards him, 'Are you not me?' The child replied, 'Maybe'.

It was precisely at that moment that Amma shook Aruna awake and said, 'Aruna, why are you lying here? Read yourself to sleep, did you? Go and eat your dosas.' Aruna felt like bursting into tears, but she went into the kitchen quietly.

When she returned the book to the library, the secretary asked her, 'How did you read this book? Didn't you want to know what happened in the end?'

Aruna was a bit shy and hesitant, but she replied, 'Indeed I wanted to, Uncle, but I saw some of the end-part in a dream.'

The secretary laughed out aloud and said, 'Then you can dream the rest of the book after you read it again, my child!'

Happy inside, Aruna told herself, 'Who knows? Maybe I will.' And then she told herself again, 'Maybe there are people who can dream a whole book!'

Translated from the Malayalam by J. Devika

the school

Ranjit Lal

When we shifted next door to the school, it was in the middle of the summer holidays, so it was naturally deserted. From our bedroom window we got a clear view of its red mud grounds and playing fields, and of the building itself, which, frankly, invited illegal exploration. It was a huge, imposing four-storey structure, gaunt and grey and square as any prison, its windows glittering blindly in the sun. Its compound was ringed by high walls and razor wire, over which we could easily see because our house stood on the higher side of the hillside. A huge black and white board, already rusting, proclaimed: 'Heaven's Gate High School', followed by what was probably the motto of the school: 'Keeping Young Hopes Alive.'

'Whoever named it must be loony!' I snorted. 'Have you seen it?' And why would anyone build a school here, God only knew. Just as why our parents had built their 'dream farmhouse' here, right at the end of a potholed road abutting the ferocious gullies of the Ridge. The road ended here; the nearest neighbour was a kilometre away (and probably a jackal). It was truly the back of beyond.

'Let's see what it's like,' my twin sister Salma said one boring morning, when it was pouring freakishly and the TV cable was down—nothing new. 'Come on, don't just sit there and gape. Get your raincoat, Sohail!' She grabbed my hand and grinned.

Salma was always like that: plunging into things head first, without thinking matters through and getting us into trouble.

'Hang on. It's illegal to trespass...'

'So who's trespassing; we're just having a look.' Her brown eyes sparkled. 'Just to see if we'd like to attend it when term starts.'

'We already have a school to go to, in case you have forgotten.'

She made a face. 'I know, but it must be the most boring school in the world! Full of those richie-rich, snot-nosed types.'

'Anyone who goes to our school must be richie-rich! You heard what Papa had to say about our fees: you could feed a thousand children for a year for a term's fee...'

'Now, are you coming or not?' She was pulling me along. Well, we were different, but we were twins, and one law of twindom was that you did things together. She'd done the same for me—as reluctantly—as I had for her. 'Okay, hang on...'

Getting in was no problem. There were several 'breaches in the defences' as Salma gleefully described them, meaning, holes in the wall. Besides, it was pouring, so there was no one around. We splashed happily through the red mud in the compound, leaving muddy footsteps up the steps to the main entrance. Salma wrung out her hair, her eyes glinting as she eyed the huge padlock on the main door. I looked around nervously. My sister was already sliding towards one of the side doors, putting her nose against the glass and peering inside. The side doors were bolted from the inside—not that this was any trouble for Salma. She dug out a large rock from a flower bed.

'Hankie!' she demanded, snatching mine and wrapping it around her hand.

'Salma! That's breaking and entering!'

Crash! Tinkle! 'Ooops!' she giggled. 'Imagine a broken window pane! We'd better check no one's trespassing inside...'

She reached inside carefully, but her fingers couldn't reach the bolt. 'Come on Sohail, it's your turn now.' We were twins, but I was taller than my sister (who bore me a grudge for this—we were supposed to be 'equal in every way', according to her).

We were in. This must be the assembly hall. It was enormous, probably taking up most of the ground floor, and it had a gleaming black and white marble floor. At one end was a stage, from where the principal no doubt made patriotic announcements and disbursed pearls of wisdom, and the class monitors stood in a virtuous row and smirked. On the walls were pictures of our national leaders—some truly great, others crooks and thugs whom we were supposed to respect.

Well, let me put it this way. Salma and I had a wonderful summer running riot in that school; we just freaked out. There was something delicious about going to a school—especially one with a name like this one's—when you were not meant to be there; and as Salma put it, 'doing what we always wanted to do with schools!'(Which was pretty much to wreck them!) Of course it would have been even better had it been our own school, but still. We'd sneak in there virtually every day, careful that we were not seen while entering. Once inside the building, we were safe. There was never a soul around—it was a bit surprising that there were no caretakers or peons or even chowkidars in the grounds. Even stray dogs, pigs and chickens gave the place a wide berth. We skated about in the empty echoing classes and corridors, and Salma perfected her skills of lock-picking, skilfully opening up classroom after classroom. We raided and rearranged their library, went through the Chemistry and Biology labs 'like bulls in a china shop', lounged about in the staff rooms and had a blast. We checked the cupboards in the classrooms and flipped through several grubby notebooks.

'Hey, look at this!' I said glancing at an essay by someone called Basudha Bhullar in X C. 'Basudha here wants to be an astronaut like Kalpana Chawla.' Salma grinned. 'And this fellow Hariram Bisht wants to be Tendulkar except that he admits he got out for a duck in his last match!'

We even rummaged through the principal's office, and in one reckless and heady moment jimmied open some locked filing cabinets. We couldn't do very much with the computers, though—they were password protected and neither of us were geeks or nerds; we could e-mail and chat and Google of course, but that was pretty much it. But a plain old cobra or box file—which you could just flip open and read—ah that was different!

'Bloody hell!' I said, scanning a file I had picked out at random. 'The bugger has personal files on individual students! Look at this!'

'Aradhana Chopra; Age 16; Class X A; Date of Admission: 12 December 2005. Good Student; Wears too much jewellery; Otherwise good discipline.' There was a passport-size photograph of a vapid-looking girl with the usual two plaits staring owlishly at the camera.

Salma's eyes were wide as saucers. 'Good grief!' she exclaimed, hands on her hips. 'And have you seen the size of the school? There must be 5,000 kids coming here. Don't tell me they have dossiers on every one of them!'

'Well, look at the number of filing cabinets. Man, this is a computer printout, so these are hard-copy backups— they've probably got a database...' She was riffling through another file. 'Hey, listen to this: Manmohan Ramanathan; Age 15; Class IX C; Date of Admission: 24 July 2003. Average Student; Attends counselling twice weekly; Discipline issues, is still picking fights; Parents recently divorced...'

We looked at each other.

Mama and Papa were not divorced, nor going to be divorced; they simply were never around—both had high-power jobs with 24x7 timings. We had more contact with them through e-mail and mobiles than in real life.

'Well, they're divorced from us!' Salma had cried angrily once, when she had gotten into trouble at school and they had been called up (and started arguing over who should come). They couldn't give a shit whether we were dead or alive!

Anyway, we had a total party in Heaven's Gate High School. By the end of the summer, we had painted graffiti on the walls. We were just lucky that the Chemistry lab didn't go up in purple flames; I don't know what we did with the computers...I doubt they'd ever work again. It just sort of happened naturally; there was no scheming or pre-planning or anything malicious on our part. Something seemed to come over us when we stepped inside that vast marble assembly hall. It just happened.

'The shit's going to hit the fan when school starts,' Salma said with a giggle, towards the end of the holidays. I'd love to be around to see what the reaction is!'

'Those names...' I frowned. 'Salma, I'm sure I've seen some of those names before...and the photographs...'

'Yes,' she giggled, 'I noticed you were checking out the pictures of some of the girls...How many did you rip off?'

'I did not!' But I had: some of the chicks in that school were real knockouts—like one called Harshita Sen, whom I'd love to meet. Even in those dumb-looking passport photographs, their beauty shone out like a beacon.

She nodded. 'But you're right. I distinctly remember the name Zafira Keswani from somewhere...Oh well... it'll come back to me sometime...'

Heaven's Gate High School opened a week before ours. On that Monday, both Salma and I catapulted out of bed as we heard the roar of cars, motorbikes and buses arriving to drop the kids. We'd never seen the kids in real life before—they wore the usual grey and white uniform, with navy blue ties, black shoes and white socks. They were just ordinary school kids—shouting, whistling, eating, fooling around, making a racket and happy to be meeting each other after the holidays, some anxiously waving their parents goodbye. The first shift lined up for assembly outside at 7.30 a.m. At the window, Salma and I took turns with the binoculars.

The principal was a short fleshy-looking woman in a flowery sari, and jasmine in her hair. She had a shrill, petulant voice, but seemed quite good-tempered. They sang *Vande Mataram*, swore an oath of allegiance (at least that's what it sounded like) and then the National Anthem was played and they yelled 'Jai Hind' and trooped inside in orderly lines.

'They must have discovered our destruction...' Salma muttered, puzzled. 'Yet the principal's one cool cat. I thought she'd be raving and ranting and frothing at the mouth.'

'Hey, Salma, do you realize, we never saw any signs of the school being prepared for opening?' I asked. 'I mean there ought to have been an army of sweepers etc., cleaning out the place, opening the windows and so on—for days before. It just opened...'

'Perhaps the kids are doing that now!' Salma snorted. 'I'd like to meet some of the kids in that school,' she said, but I knew immediately this was another idea that could get us into trouble.

Of course we wandered out at lunchtime and hung around the gates, smiling inanely as the kids thronged around the candyfloss and ice cream vendors that congregate at such places—even if they're remotely located. As I mentioned, our house and Heaven's Gate High School are pretty much at the edge of the town. There's nothing but wilderness and the Ridge beyond.

By the second day, we were nodding at some of the kids and by the third morning, we'd broken the ice. A girl with lovely grey eyes suddenly realized that she hadn't brought any money for the ice cream she had just eaten, and was almost in tears. She must have been new, because she didn't seem to have any friends—the others sort of ignored her. The ice cream vendor was getting difficult and threatening to tell the principal. By now the bell had rung and all the kids had gone back, except this girl, who was still pleading with the vendor.

'Here…I'll pay for it,' I said, gallantly. 'You can square with me tomorrow.' I paid the fellow as if I were Bill Gates. Salma grinned and nudged me. The girl was very pretty.

'Hi,' Salma introduced herself. 'I'm Salma; he's my

brother, Sohail. We live in that house. What's your name?'

'Thanks…Thanks so much. I'm Tanvi…It's my first day here…'

'Listen, if the others are jerks, you can always come over to our place…' I invited generously. She had a lovely snub nose—and again something tugged at the back of my mind. I'd seen her before somewhere…very recently…

'Haven't I seen you somewhere?'

'He's already flirting!' Salma snorted. 'But do come over whenever you want to bunk!'

By some miracle Mom came home early from work that evening and Salma tackled her headlong.

'Mom, why don't you take us out of that stupid richie-rich school we go to and put us into Heaven's Gate High School? It's next door, in case you hadn't noticed…'

Mom glanced up from her infernal Blackberry. 'Don't be silly, Salma.'

'But it makes sense! We won't have to travel for an hour up and down every day and can use the time to finish our homework properly.'

'Salma, please!'

'But why?'

Mom looked up with raised eyebrows. Oh, oh, a sarky

remark was about to be downloaded. 'In case you failed to notice, that school's been boarded up. There are locks on its gates and it's been like this ever since we moved here.'

'*What*?' This was both of us in chorus. 'Ma, you've been working too hard.'

'Look, I've had enough of this nonsense from both of you.'

That was the end of that conversation.

But next morning, Salma's case—for our changing school no matter what Mom said—was considerably strengthened. A school bus, being driven at recklessly high speed, crashed on the Gurgaon-Delhi expressway, killing twenty-three kids. We saw their pictures—on TV and the papers—with horror. They were just kids like us. We, too, drove on that highway in our school bus every day. It could have as easily been us...

'Look!' Salma said ghoulishly, smacking the paper under Mom's nose. 'This can easily happen to us—you don't know how rashly our bus driver drives!'

'Salma, please the subject is not open to discussion...' She looked irritated. 'Why don't you be like your brother and take up something sensible like birdwatching.' She'd noticed the binoculars. Ah, yes...maybe, but...

I was at the window the next morning with the binoculars, trying to see if I could spot Tanvi or even Harshita, when the bell went. I didn't want to hang around aimlessly at the gate, lest she think I only wanted my money back. But if she were there, I could—with Salma's help—'bump' into her, and of course chat her up a bit. What I saw made me forget everything...

'Salma, get over here!' I shouted hoarsely.

'What's the matter? You've gone grey!'

'L... L-look at those kids...th-that group standing near the gates...'

'They're just a bunch of kids hanging around at the gate...Oh okay...what's the matter?'

Then she saw what the matter was.

'Oh...oh my god! The school bus kids!'

They were the kids that had died the previous morning in the school bus crash! They hung around in a group, unsure of their surroundings and the other kids, very much like some nervous new kids on the block...

Salma was staring at me in horror.

'Then, you mean...'

'Salma, do you remember the names of some of those kids in the files?'

'Zafira Keswani...'

I Googled that on the computer: over 450 references. I checked one. It turned out to be a news item from an old issue of the *Hindustan Times*: Zafira Keswani, a brilliant student had been killed when she had fallen off the roof of her house. There was speculation as to whether it was suicide, accident or murder...

As for Harshita Sen, no controversy here—she'd been killed by a blow on her head dealt by her father and brother in a fit of temper after they apparently discovered she had a boyfriend...

Salma had gone pale. 'Sohail, check that first girl—Aradhana Sharma...'

I did. 'She's dead too. Died on 11 December 2005. In a bomb explosion...'

And then I remembered Tanvi...A girl called Tanvi had been run over by a car while on a pedestrian crossing, a few days ago.

'Sohail...remember the dates of admission? They were all different: all a day after they died...'

'Heaven's Gate High School...' I Googled. Over 250 references. Most were for other schools with the same name in other cities. So I keyed in the address. Mom had been right; the school had been closed for years—there was some massive property dispute going on, and the case was in court.

But...

White-faced, I keyed in my name. There were twenty-three references, none of them of any relevance. Then, Salma—she had forty-five references, and insisted I plough through the lot. Nothing. We were safe.

'Let's pay a visit to the school this Sunday,' Salma said in a small voice. 'Just to make sure...' She looked at me pleadingly. 'I mean no one sees what we're seeing. Mom thinks you've taken up birdwatching!'

This time we entered at night, feeling a bit like criminals returning to the scene of the crime. Only there was no sign of any crime—our graffiti murals had vanished, the classes were spic and span, and the test-tubes, beakers, flasks in the Chemistry lab glittered on the shelves. Again, there was no watchman, nothing. We checked around a bit and then reluctantly went to the principal's office and the filing cabinets. Salma did her little jiggling trick and they slid open.

M...N...O...P...Pat...Patel...Patil...no Patnaik... thank God...

Whew. We turned to leave, giddy with relief. As we turned to shut the door, we saw two folders on the principal's gleaming and otherwise empty desk: new ones.

On the cover of each, emblazoned in golden Gothic capitals under the name of the school, were:

Salma Patnaik.

Sohail Patnaik.

Date of admission: It was the day after tomorrow.

Inside, they were empty.

'At least,' Salma said in a small voice, her hand creeping into mine. 'At least we'll still go to school together and it'll be so near home...'

And hopefully I could chat up either Tanvi or Harshita—or both.

As we slipped back through the hole in the wall, I glanced back at the school board. The name was faded and rust-marked, but the motto had been painted over freshly: 'Keeping Young Hopes Alive!'

I clutched my sister's hand and we walked home together.

eid

Paro Anand

Ayub came home from school in tears. Although his mother asked and asked and even tried to bribe him with his favourite gajar ka halwa, he was unwilling to tell her what had happened. Or maybe, he was unable to. It worried Ammie, she just didn't know what to do.

Eventually, Ayub calmed down and sat moodily munching his halwa. She decided not to drive him further into his silence by her questions. That afternoon, she let him watch cartoons before his homework—something that happened very rarely. But she was relieved when he smiled and her heart sang out when she heard him giggle at the screen.

It was when Papa came home and they were sitting having their soup that Ayub finally came out with what was bothering him. 'Papa, are we Muslim?' he asked.

The soup went cold as Ayub told his parents about his day. About his days since the terrorist attacks in Mumbai. With the images of the Taj Hotel dome burning fresh in their minds, Ayub's classmates had started their teasing, taunting and yes, even bullying. Ayub recalled all that had been happening to him.

'It's you guys who do this every time.'

'Every time.'

'You Mossies are just killers.'

'What d'you eat for breakfast? Bodies?'

'Do you drink blood instead of milk?'

And then it had become worse. Shaan and his gang began teasing Ayub's friends, threatening them not to hang around with him any more. Every time they did, the others would pass by whispering, 'Traitor', 'gadaar' 'khalnayak'...

Eventually, only Shaurya had the guts to stick it out with Ayub.

'Just ignore them,' was his constant refrain.

But Ayub couldn't help tensing up every time there was another barb, another taunt flung his way.

But that day it had crossed all boundaries. Shaurya

wasn't in school that day, he'd gone for a tennis match. So Ayub was alone, he took his lunch box and tried to quickly go to the furthest corner of the playground. Get away before they could follow. But they'd seen him. Shaan had gathered his cronies and a whole lot of others who joined in. Many because they were too scared to say no to Shaan, but others because they actually believed that all Muslims were, in fact, terrorists, or at least sympathizers to their cause. That had been the talk in their homes, often.

They waited for Ayub to disappear behind the trees that bordered the walls.

'Good,' smirked Shaan to himself.

In fact, Ayub had made it much worse for himself. He'd not managed to escape the gaze of his tormentors, but had gone to an isolated spot where no one would see what was happening to him.

As he sat, lunch box open, but not eating, they came for him.

'Ah Mossie boy, so here you are!'

'You planning to blow up the school or something?'

'Enjoying your blood sandwich, are you?'

One of them snatched the tiffin box from his hand

and opened the sandwich. They jeered as it was crumbled and thrown to the ground. They cheered as one of them stamped on the box until it snapped and smashed. From the corner of his eye, Ayub saw that his brownie had found its way into Shaan's pocket. Ayub tried to see if there was any escape for him. Could he make a dash for it? But there were too many of them. There was no way out.

No way out when Shaan caught hold of him from the back of his head. No way out when Shaan bent him over, rubbing his nose, his face into the ground. No way out as Ayub struggled for breath as he finally, finally sobbed out, as they demanded,

'I'm sorry, I'm sorry...I am a Muslim...I am a terrorist...I'm sorry I killed so many people.'

The laughing and hooting subsided as they left him sobbing and dirty on the ground behind the trees. From far away, he'd heard the bell ring for the end of the break. But his legs were shaking too hard. He couldn't stand for a long time. Finally, he'd managed to struggle to the bathroom and wash his face. Not knowing what else to do. Knowing that there was no way he could go to the teachers and tell them what had just happened. That was out of the question. So he walked into class, late. Steeling himself for the inevitable taunting giggles that rose. And for the scolding for being late.

'Speak up! I'm asking you a question—why are you so late for class?'

He just hung his head down, knowing that his silence was incensing the teacher more and more. But there was no answer he could give, so he mumbled a sorry and hoped it would be enough.

And then, through the afternoon, he was lost in thought, wondering how he was going to persuade his parents that he had to drop out of school, or at least transfer to another one. He took more scoldings for being inattentive in his stride. That was the least of his problems.

But most of all, Ayub just couldn't figure out why they were picking on him. Was he different from all the others? And if yes, then, how?

Ayub added salty tears into the redness of his tomato soup. He couldn't bear it. He was the gentlest of children. He hated the way most boys would smack and knock each other 'just for the fun of it.' He couldn't see the fun in causing or receiving a painful whack.

He stayed clear of the rowdier boys and liked to play with girls, although he couldn't do that too much, because then the teasing became worse, he explained.

'They say, we should kill all the Muslims and only then will the world be peaceful.'

'That's what they say?' Papa and Ma looked at each other, horrified.

'Yes, and they say their parents say that too.'

Ayub's parents had always known that they would one day talk about religion with their son, but they hadn't thought it would be so soon, when he was just ten years old. They came from different religions themselves. He was Muslim and she was Christian. Neither family had accepted, or even forgiven them for falling in love. There had been bitter fights at their homes. Bordering on violence, almost.

No one from their families had attended the quiet court marriage that they'd had. They had never practised their religions after that. 'If it causes so much hatred, what good is it to go through the motions of praying to pieces of paper or stone statues?' they'd said. So they brought up their son without a religion. They celebrated birthdays, but no religious festivals. If he wanted to play Holi, or light candles at Diwali or get presents from Santa, he did. But they hadn't talked about the religious significance of what he was doing or that they were festivals of different religions.

They'd known this day would come, yet they weren't prepared at all to face it. And they hadn't imagined it would be brought up in such harsh circumstances.

They sat him down between them. They brought out family albums. Long ago ones that had his parents each of them as children. Each of them showing the religions of their backgrounds. 'This is a cross, beta, there is a story about how the Lord Jesus Christ was crucified on it because of his beliefs.'

'This is my first Eid, see how proud everyone is. I was the first son.'

And they explained to him that officially he was half Muslim and half Christian. You have the best of two worlds, you know.

But the questions still remained. Why was he being taunted? And what did being half and half make him?

And when they had said all that could be said about it, Ayub asked, 'So I am Christian and I am Muslim and that's okay? And I'm not going to be a killer, am I?' His very last question is what shook them the most, 'Why didn't you ever tell me about my religion before, were you ashamed of it?'

Ayub's parents knew that they were going to have to do something about it. Although he begged them not to, they went to school. They talked with the class teacher, the principal and some others. They were horrified too at what had happened. Like most schools, this one had left the question of religion and discussion around it out of the curriculum. Out of the assembly prayers even, where they chose non-religious prayers for the general good of mankind. Policies they thought would be correct and healing and not bring about any conflict. But it hadn't turned out that way. At all.

The classes were addressed. The teachers thought it best to take a direct approach. Rather than just suspending the children, they wanted to try and convince them. Ayub's parents agreed. So now they stood before the class, the parents and teachers and principal together.

Ayub was nervous. Would his friends laugh? Would they be rude to him again? Or to his parents? Would they understand at all? Ayub's parents were worried, too. Had they done the right thing in not talking about all of this earlier? Had they talked of it too soon? Would their son and his classmates really be able to comprehend all that they were about to say about such a complex thing as religion, and the similarities and differences? That religion only ever taught you to be a good human being? There was no religion that said you had to be a killer. There were bad people in any religion who killed and used their faith as an excuse. Therefore it didn't matter what religion you were born with. One or more. Or any, for that matter.

One by one, they all read passages from different holy books—the Bible, the Koran, the Guru Granth Sahib, the Bhagvad Gita and the Upanishads. They also talked about some of the difficulties they'd faced, being from different religions. About how they'd come to be so wary that, in fact, they'd never even shared with their own son what his religion was. That they celebrated festivals of all religions, but never talked about their religious significance, because they felt that it had started to breed violence and hatred in the world.

The class shifted uneasily. Shaan hung his head as others were glancing at him. He'd often picked on other kids, for all kinds of reasons. But he'd never had to face such a direct approach. He felt the reproach rise within him. For himself.

And he could barely believe his ears when Ayub's mother extended the invitation. He looked up to see her smile at him as she said, 'So, we'd like to invite all of you to an Eid party. It will be Ayub's first official Eid. Here are the cards. We'd be very happy if your parents came too. I do hope that all of you will come.'

Finally, Ayub was dressed in his new white kurta pyjama. He wore his thread skull cap and he said his morning prayer on his brand new prayer mat. Kneeling alongside his father, watching from the corner of his eye as he bent forward and laid his forehead on the mat, facing in the direction of Mecca.

Then he'd helped both his parents put the silver foil on the kheer, put raisins into the sevian. Put crisp notes of money into the new white envelopes for his friends' Eidi that he'd decorated himself.

Now it was time for the party to start.

When the first car drove up, Ayub felt almost faint with surprise, joy and terror. But his mother held his shoulder and gave him a small secret squeeze. They opened the door together to start celebrating Ayub's first Eid.

pinty's soap

Sanjay Khati

Such a thing had never occurred in our village before. Many of us had heard about 'soap', but there could hardly be two or three who had actually set eyes on it. If people were aware of the existence of soap at all, it was thanks to some army men. Also because when Deputy Saheb's daughter visited the village once, some women observed this object with her. It was said that wherever Pinty might be standing, a scent of flowers surrounded her up to a distance of at least two miles. If ten or fifteen years later people still had memories of that Pinty, it was because of soap. People would place it in the category of fragrance, behind attar and other such perfumes.

Well, Pinty was a being who had arrived from another world. Soap had never been glimpsed with any other person in the village. In truth, I was the one who acquired the first cake of soap in our village. That too, in a sudden, unexpected manner.

It was the fifteenth of August or some such special day, because school was closed. Kaka and I had walked several miles to sell potatoes in a small town. My uncle must have been five or six years older than me. We were almost like friends. Sometimes though, in view of his age he did display an eagerness to throw his weight around. However, he never succeeded in his attempts to assert authority over me.

We were roaming around, sucking lemon drops, enthralled by the razzle-dazzle of the town, when we arrived at a crowded field. The place was as packed as a fairground. Extremely noisy as well. Whistles were being blown and a man's authoritative voice was booming over a loudspeaker, as if scolding everyone.

Confused, quite oblivious, we were burrowing deeper into the crowd when I suddenly found myself lined up in a row of boys, similar to me in age. Someone had caught hold of my arm and hurriedly made me stand there. A man was marshalling everyone, making them take up position near a white line. On either side of me boys were yelling, flexing one leg as if getting ready to pounce on something, over and over again.

It appeared that a race was about to begin.

At first I got scared. I looked around for Kaka but could not trace him. The men who stood there brandishing sticks must have shoved him away with the rest of the crowd. The loudspeaker was intoning numbers.

One...two

And three! They all dashed off like starving beasts. I along with them. At first I couldn't figure out what to do, but when I noticed the boy next to me racing ahead pumping his matchstick legs, I pelted after him like a fury. With such force that in no time at all I got entangled in the rope stretched across the other end of the field and fell down. It was another matter that I hurt my knee too, slightly. When I dusted myself off and rose, the sound of clapping resounded in my ears. And a shiny box was thrust into my hands.

A giggling Kaka emerged from somewhere in the crowd. The two of us laughed and laughed. I was itching to run some more. Run and run. I bounded ahead and Kaka followed me, panting away. We left the town behind. I was racing pell-mell towards the village when Kaka began to call out to me. Eventually, when I came to a halt near the river, he caught hold of me.

'What's going on?' he asked.

Then I remembered that I was still clutching the shiny red box. Immediately, Kaka grabbed it and began to examine it, turning it over in his hands. He was the one who guessed that it was a cake of soap. His face was beginning to gleam with excitement. He sniffed it again and again. When I asked him for it, he wouldn't give it back.

'I'm not eating it up!' he snapped. His intentions did not seem honest.

I flared up. After all, it belonged to me. I tried to snatch it back. Struggled to knock him over. But it was impossible to get the better of that ruffian—tall and strapping as he was. By now he had opened up the gleaming wrapper and taken out the delicate pink cake that lay within.

I resorted to my ultimate weapon. I dropped down on the rocks near the river with a resounding thud. And began to bawl, shedding real tears. 'I'll tell Ija…!'

The trick worked, as it always did. Kaka glared at me with reddened eyes, then flung the cake of soap at me, saying, 'Go, die.' I leapt at it. 'Give me the wrapper too!'

Kaka threw the wrapper at me. I wrapped the fragile cake carefully in the wrapper and made my way home, laughing, sniffing at it.

Thus was launched a serious antagonism between us, the first ever. At that time I was so absorbed in the delicate scent of the soap that I had no time to take notice of Kaka. Later, this animosity became permanent.

Well, that evening, Kaka walked behind me kicking stones. The moment we reached home, he cocked his head and announced, 'Gopiya's head is so high in the air today that he can't even glance down. Just because he got a cake of soap.'

Ija was gathering the cow dung into a heap. She stood up and said, '*Saban*! Where did you get it? What is it like? Show it to me!'

'It's mine!' I snapped.

Ija went and washed her hands clean. 'Show it. Let me see too, what kind of soap it is.'

But I had no faith left in anyone. After much fussing, when I opened my fingers, Ija picked it up with great delight. She went close to the lamp and examined it carefully. Then sniffed it two or three times. 'I'll bathe with it,' she said.

I swooped on it like a bird of prey. Grabbed it and stuffed it into an inside pocket. Ran and stood at a distance of least twenty footsteps. Ija could only gape. 'Go die,' she said furiously. 'May your soap burn up!' She walked off, glaring at me.

So, that's how my mother became enemy number two. The truth was—I was unable to grasp the consequence of this cake of soap. I was too young, perhaps. But soon I began to get the feeling that I was surrounded by foes. I knew it—that Kaka turned all my belongings inside out. That he inspected each and every canister and tin that existed in our house.

To the extent that he sifted the hay and straw in the cowshed. But no one was able to ascertain where the soap was kept—except me.

Beaten, Kaka tried flattery. But I was no longer so gullible.

Bapu wasn't lucky enough to see the soap. Ija and Kaka had provoked him so much by harping on it constantly that he resorted to violence. However, by now I was well aware that temptation would strike anyone who happened to even glance at it. So I wouldn't budge from my stand. Defeated, Bapu gave me a couple of kicks, saying, 'So...

he's acquired a taste for perfume and scent! Make him take the cows out to graze!'

I did not shed a single tear and swallowed the insult. However, from that very moment I began to doubt that he was my real father.

My sister Kunti did get the opportunity to touch and smell the soap, under my strict supervision. Since then, she follows me around, wide eyed. There's no way to get rid of her, apart from giving her a couple of tight slaps.

With so many people around me, it was becoming hard for me to look at the soap again and again, the way I wanted to. My restlessness grew. Each day felt like a mountain that had to be climbed. Finally, on Sunday I made a tough decision and took out the soap, got some hot water and sat down to bathe.

This would be my first bath with the soap. I removed the paper casing lovingly. Placed it carefully in the sun. Held the soap tenderly in my right hand and touched it lightly to my wet hair.

The pink cake had some letters engraved on it. I did not know how to read English but whatever was written added greatly to the beauty of the soap. I had to take care that the letters didn't get rubbed out.

Kaka ostensibly sat inside studying but his head would keep popping up at the window. In between I could hear him read loudly from his book. On her way to cut grass for fodder, Ija halted in the middle of the courtyard. She watched me for a while then pulled a face and left. Kunti stood two steps away and gazed entranced at the soap sliding on my head, the white foam emerging from it and the multi-coloured bubbles glistening in the sun.

'Scram! Get lost!'

Kunti began to plead, 'Dada, give me a little too!'

I knew Kunti too well. She was as sly as a cat. It was best to chase her away. First I threw water at her. When she didn't budge, I slapped her with my wet hands. The moment she fled, screaming, Kaka came clattering down the stairs. 'You raised your hand on her? You're going to get it today!' But he did not move beyond the fence. Just stood there and glared. I was too far off. I continued to enjoy myself, whipping up foam, laughing. Kaka kept hurling abuses but did not go away.

I rubbed myself with the soap for a long time then poured water on my body. Dried out the soap. It had not worn out noticeably. I placed it back in its covering. Then I swaggered past Kaka. He sniffed the air.

How fresh my body felt. What a delightful scent! And how soft my hair felt! I quickly got dressed, worried that the fragrance might escape.

~

I used to leap off the parapet that surrounded our courtyard and often I'd begin to fly. I'd float like the pigeons above the high, high mountains, forests, far, far away. How many lands, how many villages would slip away beneath me! My body would tingle all over. When I looked down, our house appeared tiny, like a toy. And Ija, Bapu, Kaka, Kunti, all the people, how different they looked—like ants. I would soar high above the whole world. Everything would be below me. Nobody could reach me.

They say that when they're growing, children dream of flying. But dreams are not reality, someone also said.

After bathing with soap that day, I felt I could take off any moment.

I had school that day. Early in the morning, I worked up a fine lather and scrubbed myself till I shone. I dressed my perfumed body in my best clothes. Parted my hair with great care. All the way, I kept lifting up my elbow, sniffing at it to make sure the fragrance had not evaporated. No, fragrance doesn't evaporate. It lasts for hours. If there were no sunshine, no sweat, if dust didn't fly and the wind didn't blow, perhaps your body would always exude fragrance.

It took the class by storm. Soon all the boys had their noses pointing up, sniffing the air crazily. For a while I enjoyed the scene, smiling faintly. Then I placed my arm straight on the face of the boy sitting next to me.

'Oh, baba ho! What have you put on?' The boy actually jumped. The class was thrown into such a welter of confusion that God forbid it should ever happen again. Pushing, shoving, the boys sprang at me and dug their noses wherever they could to get a whiff. Those who were done pushed their eyeballs right up to their hairlines and began to cry, 'Tell us! Tell us!'

And when, enjoying myself thoroughly, I told them the whole story, the room was filled with clamour. 'Is it true? There's a covering along with it? But it will finish one day, then? Then what, he'll take part in the race again and win another. It'll last a year at least. Show it, yaar, come on.'

When Massa'ab arrived the noise was stilled. But

none of them could concentrate on their lessons. They were all watching me, from the corners of their eyes. I was soaring really high in the sky now. That moment if I had proclaimed that I was the monitor from now on, they would all have said, 'Yes, you are!' They had heard about Pinty from their elders, about her soap. Finding that dream-like story coming true, they were going wild.

The bell rang for half time. The boys got up to dash out as usual. Then suddenly all of them froze. I was still seated in my place. 'Come on, come!' Today all of them wanted to stick close to me. Even those who used to beat me up, taking advantage of my skinniness.

I rose, but an unfamiliar reluctance besieged me. This had never happened before. Earlier, I was invariably the first among those in a hurry to rush out. But then the boys had never surrounded me and said, 'Come, come on,' either.

'You're on our side'. 'No, on ours.' A furious battle flared up to determine which side I'd be on to play kabaddi.

I was overcome with constraint. The thought of being chased around in the game of kabaddi, rolling in the mud, was terrifying. 'No, I don't want to play,' I said.

'Why? Why?' The shouts came at me from all sides. Then all of a sudden it seemed as if the boys had understood. 'All right, you'll be the referee. You can sit and watch.' They all moved away, frustrated.

~

Word had spread through the village like wildfire. Each and everyone was dying to take a look at the soap. People would stop me on the way. Find some excuse for visiting us. They wanted me to show them the soap. When I refused, they would get annoyed. Even scold me. All the same, they would definitely sniff at me. My family must have faced some embarrassment on my account. Later on, *they* would make me the target of their abuses. Kaka would always make threatening gestures. A couple of times, finding me alone, he squeezed my throat. Kunti was forever sulking. If I ever happened to quarrel with her, Bapu would lose no time in letting me experience the weight of his two and a half kilo hand. Ija always spoke to me in an irritated tone.

The whole world seemed as rapacious as vultures trying to snatch away this tiny modicum of joy from my life. I noticed that in the beginning people would be very deferential, but when I didn't show them the soap they would immediately turn hostile. Almost everyone had become my enemy now.

People even nicknamed me Pinty. This was not a joke. It was a way of showing their loathing. The boys would call out, 'Pinty, Pinty!' And the most astonishing thing was that despite feeling troubled by this I began to wonder where Pinty was and what she was like. I even sketched an outline in my mind, which I would fill up with colour in my spare time. I believed that she must look like the goddess Lakshmi on our calendar. She was as fair skinned and her clothes were so shiny that a glow surrounded her even in the darkness of the night. Not a single speck of dust could settle on her. She was as light as if created out of a blank, white sheet of paper.

And I had abandoned all play. Some of the boys did want to keep me company but the allure of living it up with the group would draw them away. When they were enjoying their noisy games, I would sit on the low wall, shaking my legs. They would chase each other playing kabaddi, rush into the clammy fields to search for cucumbers, steal lemons, bathe in the river with their clothes off, and slide on the dry pine needles. They would shriek and yell, wrestle, tear their clothes or scrape their bodies the way they always did. I would watch them from my seat, cracking my knuckles.

The truth is, I often longed to jump into the midst of the group. But whenever I was about to do this, God knows what made my body freeze. At such moments I wished that someone would just drag me from my seat and shove me on to the field where they were playing kabaddi. But perhaps this was not possible. Now they didn't even ask me to join them. They had all accepted that Pinty's role was to sit and watch. They had begun to forget my real identity.

Now Kaka was setting off to market. He was gathering bags to carry stuff back in. I couldn't control myself. 'I'm coming too,' I said.

Kaka flared up. 'You will not come with me.'

'I will.'

'Bhabhi!' Kaka proclaimed, 'Ask him to get your stuff. I'm not going.'

Ija charged at me like a tigress. She caught hold of my ear and hurled me to the ground. 'I'm going to settle you today. The bigger he's growing, the more rotten he's getting.' She gave me a couple of kicks on my back and dragged me out.

Kaka yelled out enthusiastically from behind, 'Fix Pinty well and proper.'

Ija dragged me like a dead rat to the parapet and pushed me into a bed of nettles—'Oh I-ija...Ve...'

One last fragile thread of attachment had lingered. That too snapped, at that moment. At half time in school, as I sat on the low wall, my eyes filled up again and again. The leaping, prancing boys began to tremble in my gaze. My body still throbbed with the agony of its encounter with the stinging nettles. My elbows were grazed, my hair full of dust. I had bathed that morning too. But not a whiff of fragrance remained on my body.

I felt like a wholehearted good cry. I'd leave; I'd depart this place! Go away forever to the land where Pinty lived. People were not like this out there. There was no hatred. None of this undeserved persecution.

And I made up my mind that as soon as I got the chance I'd run off to the market town. They said that buses left for distant places from there. I'd get on to any one. Then I'd never come back. Never.

After that moment, my resolve began to gather strength. I selected the clothes I'd take with me. I hid away a bag too, to carry them in. Collected some walnuts and spied out the place from where it was possible to help myself to some money. Now, I just waited for the right opportunity.

And once everything was in place, disaster struck.

I was bathing. No matter how cold it might be, I wouldn't miss my bath. Little did I know that Kaka was lying in wait. The moment I put down the soap he pounced on it like a cat. I was stunned. Kaka's hand was on the soap. He was picking it up when it slipped out and fell far away. By that time I had screwed up my eyes and flung a heavy brass pot at him.

Kaka cried out, 'Hai!' He swayed and sat down heavily, holding his head.

By that time I had picked up the soap and gotten ready to strike again, lota in hand. But Kaka didn't rise. Now my legs turned shaky. I shook him and said, 'Kaka, Kaka!'

He groaned, lifted his head and I saw red blood flowing from his forehead. 'You hit me!' Kaka began to mumble God knows what. Then he staggered out, still holding his head with his hands. At the threshold, he paused. Tearful face. Blood-streaked cheeks with tears gushing down. 'One day your soap will wear out,' he sobbed.

Kaka left and I stood there dazed. I opened my hand and gazed at the beautiful pink cake. How slender it looked! Its fragrance had vanished too, now.

My heart plummeted.

There was no time to cry. I quickly put on my clothes and ran upstairs. Pulled out the bag. Stuffed some clothes inside it. No time to keep the walnuts. My school bag? Why would I need it? Money?

Then I overheard Kaka tell an anxious Ija how he slipped on some cow dung and his head struck the threshold of the cowshed.

I couldn't stand straight after that. Just fell face down on my bed. After a long time I was able to get up and hide the soap in its usual place. When I returned I went off to sleep in a dark corner. Didn't even get up in the evening. Said I had a stomachache.

When I woke the next morning I found a strange light filling the place. It had snowed during the night. I hadn't even noticed it. My heart plunged with anxiety.

I rushed out barefoot on the freshly fallen snow. Who was bothered about the cold? The pile of straw was covered with four inches of snow. Here lay—my secret. When I dug out the snow with my hands I found nothing but slush beneath. Soon it was all over my fingers.

Where was my soap? Not here, nor here? Not even there?

My hands encountered something slimy. A lump of pink sludge. Scented. I sank down on the snow with a thud, the lump enclosed in my hand.

'Haria!' It was Ija. She had come to milk the cow. I looked up. Her lips were puckering up as if for a joke. The lump slipped out of my hand. A kind of sob emerged from Ija's mouth—'Haria...'

A shudder shook my entire frame, tearing me apart. Letting myself fall apart completely, I clutched my mother with my muddy hands and bawled.

Ma sat down beside me too. She gathered me close to her heart. And hiding my face in her womb warmth, I wept after a long time. The way I used to before.

And suddenly I felt as if a huge mound of ice was melting. My heart turned as light as cotton wool, turned lighter and lighter. If at that moment, a gust of wind had touched me, I would surely have taken flight.

Translated from the Hindi by Deepa Agarwal

the portrait of a lady

Khushwant Singh

My grandmother, like everybody's grandmother, was an old woman. She had been old and wrinkled for the twenty years that I had known her. People said that she had once been young and pretty and had even had a husband, but that was hard to believe. My grandfather's portrait hung above the mantelpiece in the drawing room. He wore a big turban and loose-fitting clothes. His long white beard covered the best part of his chest and he looked at least a hundred years old. He did not look the sort of person who would have a wife or children. He looked as if he could only have lots and lots of grandchildren. As for my grandmother being young and pretty, the thought was almost revolting. She often told us of the games she used to play as a child.

That seemed quite absurd and undignified on her part and we treated it like the fables of the Prophets she used to tell us.

She had always been short and fat and slightly bent. Her face was a criss-cross of wrinkles running from everywhere to everywhere. No, we were certain she had always been as we had known her. Old, so terribly old that she could not have grown older, and had stayed at the same age for twenty years. She could never have been pretty; but she was always beautiful. She hobbled about the house in spotless white with one hand resting on her waist to balance her stoop and the other telling the beads of her rosary. Her silver locks were scattered untidily over her pale, puckered face, and her lips constantly moved in inaudible prayer. Yes, she was beautiful. She was like the winter landscape in the mountains, an expanse of pure white serenity breathing peace and contentment.

My grandmother and I were good friends. My parents left me with her when they went to live in the city and we were constantly together. She used to wake me up in the morning and get me ready for school. She said her morning prayer in a monotonous sing-song while she bathed and dressed me in the hope that I would listen and get to know it by heart. I listened because I loved her voice but never bothered to learn it. Then she would fetch my wooden slate which she had already washed and plastered with yellow chalk, a tiny earthen ink pot and a reed pen, tie them all in a bundle and hand it to me. After a breakfast of a thick, stale chapatti with a little butter and sugar spread on it, we went to school. She carried several stale chapattis with her for the village dogs.

My grandmother always went to school with me because the school was attached to the temple. The priest taught us the alphabet and the morning prayer. While the children sat in rows on either side of the veranda singing the alphabet or the prayer in a chorus, my grandmother sat inside reading the scriptures. When we had both finished, we would walk back together. This time the village dogs would meet us at the temple door. They followed us to our home growling and fighting each other for the chapattis we threw to them.

When my parents were comfortably settled in the city, they sent for us. That was a turning point in our friendship.

Although we shared the same room, my grandmother no longer came to school with me. I used to go to an

English school in a motor bus. There were no dogs in the streets and she took to feeding sparrows in the courtyard of our city house.

As the years rolled by we saw less of each other. For some time she continued to wake me up and get me ready for school. When I came back she would ask me what the teacher had taught me. I would tell her English words and little things of western science and learning, the law of gravity, Archimedes' principle, the world being round, etc. This made her unhappy. She could not help me with my lessons. She did not believe in the things they taught at the English school and was distressed that there was no teaching about God and the scriptures. One day I announced that we were being given music lessons. She was very disturbed. To her music had lewd associations. It was the monopoly of harlots and beggars and not meant for gentlefolk. She rarely talked to me after that.

When I went up to university, I was given a room of my own. The common link of friendship was snapped. My grandmother accepted her seclusion with resignation. She rarely left her spinning wheel to talk to anyone. From sunrise to sunset she sat by her wheel spinning and reciting prayers. Only in the afternoon she relaxed for a while to feed the sparrows. While she sat in the veranda breaking the bread into little bits, hundreds of little birds collected round her creating a veritable bedlam of chirrupings. Some came and perched on her legs, others on her shoulders. Some even sat on her head. She smiled but never shoo'd them away. It used to be the happiest half-hour of the day for her.

When I decided to go abroad for further studies, I was sure my grandmother would be upset. I would be away for five years, and at her age one could never tell. But my grandmother could. She was not even sentimental. She came to leave me at the railway station but did not talk or show any emotion. Her lips moved in prayer, her mind was lost in prayer. Her fingers were busy telling the beads of her rosary. Silently she kissed my forehead, and when I left I cherished the moist imprint as perhaps the last sign of physical contact between us.

But that was not so. After five years I came back home and was met by her at the station. She did not look a day older. She still had no time for words, and while she clasped me in her arms I could hear her reciting her prayer. Even on the first day of my arrival, her happiest moments were with her sparrows whom she fed longer and with frivolous rebukes.

In the evening a change came over her. She did not pray. She collected the women of the neighbourhood, got an old drum and started to sing. For several hours she thumped the sagging skins of the dilapidated drum and sang of the homecoming of warriors. We had to persuade her to stop to avoid overstraining. That was the first time since I had known her that she did not pray.

The next morning she was taken ill. It was a mild fever and the doctor told us that it would go. But my grandmother thought differently. She told us that her end was near. She said that, since only a few hours before the close of the last chapter of her life she had omitted to pray, she was not going to waste any more time talking to us.

We protested. But she ignored our protests. She lay peacefully in bed praying and telling her beads. Even before we could suspect, her lips stopped moving and the rosary fell from her lifeless fingers. A peaceful pallor spread on her face and we knew that she was dead.

We lifted her off the bed and, as is customary, laid her on the ground and covered her with a red shroud. After a few hours of mourning we left her alone to make arrangements for her funeral.

In the evening we went to her room with a crude stretcher to take her to be cremated. The sun was setting and had lit her room and veranda with a blaze of golden light. We stopped halfway in the courtyard. All over the veranda and in her room right up to where she lay dead and stiff wrapped in the red shroud, thousands of sparrows sat scattered on the floor. There was no chirping. We felt sorry for the birds and my mother fetched some bread for them. She broke it into little crumbs, the way my grandmother used to, and threw it to them. The sparrows took no notice of the bread. When we carried my grandmother's corpse off, they flew away quietly. Next morning the sweeper swept the bread crumbs into the dustbin.

notes on contributors

Satyajit Ray was one of India's best-known filmmakers. He won numerous national and international awards for his films. He was also a fiction writer, publisher, illustrator, calligrapher, graphic designer and film critic. He authored several short stories and novels for young readers and created characters like Feluda, the sleuth, and Professor Shonku, the scientist. He also edited the Bengali children's magazine *Sandesh,* started by his grandfather, Upendrakishore Ray.

Gopa Majumdar has translated the works of several well-known writers like Bibhutibhushan Bandopadhyay, Ashapurna Devi, Nabaneeta Dev Sen and Satyajit Ray.

Rabindranath Tagore is the most revered figure in the field of Indian literature. He was the first non-European to win the Nobel Prize for Literature in 1913. Tagore began to write in early childhood and penned numerous novels, poems, plays and essays. Many of his works were written for children. He created a new musical form—Rabindra Sangeet and composed the national anthems of two countries, India and Bangladesh. He was passionate about education and set up the famous university at Shantiniketan.

Radha Chakravarty's translations include *Crossings: Stories from Bangladesh and India, Chokher Bali, Farewell Song: Shesher Kabita, Boyhood Days, Gora* among many others. She has also compiled and edited *Bodymaps: Stories by South Asian Women Writers*. She was nominated for the Crossword Translations Award 2004.

R.K. Narayan is credited with bringing Indian literature in English to the rest of the world, and is regarded as one of India's greatest English language novelists. *Swami and Friends* is one of his early works. He received the Sahitya Akademi Award for *The Guide* which was also made into a famous movie. Narayan also received the Padma Vibhushan, among other important awards.

Sudha Murty is a well-known social worker and writer. She has written several books among which *How I Taught My Grandmother to Read & Other Stories* has been translated into fifteen languages. Her latest book is *The Day I Stopped Drinking Milk*. Other notable books are *Wise and Otherwise, The Old Man and His God* and *Gently Falls the Bakula*. Among other awards, she has received the R.K. Narayan Award for Literature and the Padma Shri in 2006.

Sukumar Ray was a writer, editor, illustrator, photographer and printer. He is considered to be the pre-eminent writer of nonsense in India. While studying at Presidency College, Kolkata, Sukumar launched the Nonsense Club, a platform for acting, literature and general absurdity. In 1915, after his father's death, he took over the editorship of *Sandesh*, a highly regarded children's magazine, while continuing to write plays, essays and short stories and illustrating them. Many of his works like the poetry collection *Abol Tabol* (Gibberish), novella *HaJaBaRaLa* (Mumbo-Jumbo), short story collection *Pagla Dashu* (Crazy Dashu) and play *Chalachittachanchari* are still highly popular.

Sampurna Chattarji is a poet, fiction-writer and translator with eight books to her credit. Her books for children include *The Greatest Stories Ever Told* (Puffin, 2004), *Mulla Nasruddin* (Puffin, 2008), *Three Brothers and the Flower of Gold* (Scholastic, 2008) and *The Fried Frog and Other Funny Freaky Foodie Feisty Poems* (Scholastic, 2009).

Premchand was a highly influential Hindustani writer of the early twentieth century, whose works span both Hindi and Urdu. Born Dhanpat Rai, he began writing under the pen name Nawab Rai, but subsequently switched to Premchand. His works include more than a dozen novels, around 250 short stories, several essays and translations of a number of foreign literary works into Hindi. *Godaan, Nirmala* and *Gaban* are some of his famous novels.

Rakhshanda Jalil is a well-known writer, translator and editor who has translated many important works from Urdu including a collection of Saadat Hasan Manto's stories *Naked Voices: Stories and Sketches*. Her collection of short stories *Release and Other Stories* was published by HarperCollins in 2011.

K. Shankar Pillai, better known as **Shankar**, made a huge contribution to Indian children's literature. He launched Shankar's International Children's Competition in 1949, and Shankar's On-the-Spot Painting Competition for Children in 1952. Children's Book Trust, a publishing house dedicated to children's books is one of his most notable contributions. Founded in 1957, Shankar wrote and illustrated many of its most memorable titles and groomed many writers and illustrators. To foster indigenous children's literature he instituted an annual Competition for Writers of Children's Books in 1978. He was awarded the Padma Vibhushan in 1976.

Ruskin Bond has been writing for over sixty years, and has now over 120 titles in print—novels, collections of stories, poetry, essays, anthologies and books for children. His first novel, *The Room on the Roof*, received the prestigious John Llewellyn Rhys award in 1957. He has also received the Padma Shri, and two awards from the Sahitya Akademi—one for his short stories and another for his writings for children. In 2012, the Delhi government gave him its Lifetime Achievement award.

Vikram Seth is one of India's most celebrated novelists and poets. Among his best known works are *A Suitable Boy*, *The Golden Gate*, *An Equal Music*, *From Heaven Lake: Travels Through Sinkiang and Tibet* and poetry collections *Mappings* and *All You who Sleep Tonight*. Some of the many awards he has received are the Commonwealth Poetry Prize for *All You who Sleep Tonight*, the Commonwealth Writers' Prize and the W.H. Smith Literary Award for *A Suitable Boy* as well as the Crossword Book Award for *An Equal Music*. He has also been honoured with the Padma Shri.

Sundara Ramaswamy is considered one of the giants of Tamil modern literature. He edited and published a notable literary magazine called *Kalachuvadu* and wrote poetry under the pen name Pasuvayya. Among his noted works are his poetry collection *Nadunisi Naaykal* (Dogs at Midnight) and novels *Oru Puliya Marathin Kathai* (The Story of a Tamarind Tree), *J.J Silakuripukal* (J.J: Some Jottings) and *Kuzhanthaikal, Penkal, Aankal* (Children, Women, Men).

Ashokamitran, one of Tamil literature's most influential figures, began his literary career with the prize-winning play *Anbin Parisu,* followed by many short stories, novellas and novels. A distinguished essayist and critic, he is the editor of the literary journal *Kanaiyaazhi.* Most of his works have been translated into English.

Edward James 'Jim' Corbett was a British hunter-turned-conservationist, author and naturalist, famous for hunting a large number of man-eaters in the Uttarakhand region. Corbett was an avid photographer and writer. He authored classics like *Man-Eaters of Kumaon, Jungle Lore, My India* and other books recounting his hunts and experiences, which enjoyed much critical acclaim.

Paul Zacharia is a well-known Malayalam writer. Many of his short stories and novels have been translated into English and other languages. *Bhaskara Pattelar and Other Stories, Reflections of a Hen in Her Last Hour and Other Stories, Praise the Lord and What's New, Pilate?: Two Novellas* are among his famous works. He has received the Sahitya Akademi Award as well as the Katha award.

J. Devika teaches and researches at Centre for Development Studies, Thiruvananthapuram, Kerala, She translates from Malayalam to English and back. Her published translations include the works of K. R. Meera, Sarah Joseph and Nalini Jameela.

Ranjit Lal is the author of twenty-five books for children and adults, including *The Crow Chronicles, The Life and Times of Altu Faltu, The Battle for No. 19* and *Faces in the Water* for which he won the Vodafone-Crossword Children's Award 2010. *Faces in* *the Water* was also on the IBBY (International Board on Books for Young People) Honour List 2012. His stories and articles have been published in over fifty newspapers and magazines in India and abroad.

Paro Anand is a writer, performance storyteller and children's literature activist. She has authored many books for children and young adults, including plays, short stories and novels. She headed the National Centre for Children's Literature at the National Book Trust. Her book *No Guns at my Son's Funeral* was on the IBBY Honor List In 2006, *The Little Bird Who Held the Sky Up with His Feet* is on *1001 Books to Read Before You Grow Up*—a list of the world's best books of all time.

Sanjay Khati works as a journalist in Delhi. He has published two short story collections: *Pinty ka Sabun* (Pinty's Soap) and *Bahar Kuchch Naheen Tha* (There was Nothing Outside). *Pinty ka Sabun* is widely acknowledged as an important contribution to contemporary Hindi writing. The book has been awarded and many of the stories translated into various languages.

Khushwant Singh is a famous Indian novelist and journalist. He has been the editor of important magazines like *The Illustrated Weekly* and newspapers like *The Hindustan Times*. *A Train to Pakistan* is his best-known novel. He has also written many works on Sikh history. Singh's weekly column, 'With Malice towards One and All', carried by several Indian newspapers, is among the most widely-read columns in the country.

acknowledgements

Grateful acknowledgment is made to the following for permission to reprint copyright material:

Penguin Books India for 'The Vicious Vampire' by Satyajit Ray, translated by Gopa Majumdar, from *One Dozen Stories*, New Delhi: Penguin Books India, 2008

Penguin Books India for 'The Parrot's Tale' by Rabindranath Tagore, translated by Radha Chakravarty from *The Land of Cards: Stories, Poems and Plays for Children*, New Delhi: Penguin Books India, 2010

Indian Thought Publications for the extract from *Swami and Friends* by R.K. Narayan, Mysore: Indian Thought Publications, 1944

Sudha Murty for 'How I Taught My Grandmother to Read' by Sudha Murty, from *How I Taught My Grandmother to Read and Other Stories*, New Delhi: Penguin Books India, 2004

Michael Heyman, Anushka Ravishankar and Sumanyu Satpathy for 'Mister Owl and Missus' by Sukumar Ray from *The Tenth Rasa: An Anthology of Indian Nonsense*, New Delhi: Penguin Books India, 2007 and 'Pumpkin-Grumpkin' by Sukumar Ray from *Wordygurdyboom: The Nonsense World of Sukumar Ray*, New Delhi: Penguin Books India, 2011, published here in translation by Sampurna Chattarji

Children's Book Trust for 'Rain-making' from *Life with Grandfather* by Shankar, New Delhi: Children's Book Trust, 1965

Ruskin Bond for 'Here Comes Mr Oliver' by Ruskin Bond from *The Parrot Who Wouldn't Talk and Other Stories*, New Delhi: Penguin Books India, 2008

Penguin Books India for 'Big Brother' by Premchand, translated by Rakhshanda Jalil, from *A Winter's Night and Other Stories*, New Delhi: Penguin Books India, 2007

Vikram Seth for 'The Goat and the Ram' from *Beastly Tales from Here and There* by Vikram Seth, New Delhi: Penguin Books India, 1992

National Book Trust, India for 'The Stamp Album' by Sundara Ramaswamy, translated by Ashokamitran, from *The Best Thirteen*, New Delhi: National Book Trust, India, 1983

Oxford University Press, India for 'The Thak Man-eater' by Jim Corbett from *Man-eaters of Kumaon*, New Delhi: Oxford University Press, 1988

Paul Zacharia for 'The Library' translated by J. Devika, Thiruvananthapuram: Kerala State Institute of Children's Literature

Ranjit Lal for 'The School', previously published in *The Puffin Book of Spooky Ghost Stories*, New Delhi: Penguin Books India

Penguin Books India for 'Eid' by Paro Anand from *Wild Child and Other Stories*, New Delhi: Penguin Books India, 2011; also previously published in *Eid Stories*, New Delhi: Scholastic India, 2010

Sanjay Khati for 'Pinty's Soap' translated by Deepa Agarwal, from *Pinty ka Sabun*, New Delhi: Kitabghar Prakashan 1996

Khushwant Singh for 'The Portrait of a Lady' from *Book of Unforgettable Women*, New Delhi: Penguin Books India, 2000